COZY MYSTERIES FOR SUMMER

DAISY LANDISH

Editing by Jessica McKenna
Cover by Daisy Landish

BEACHES AND TRAILS
PUBLISHING

ABOUT THE AUTHOR

Daisy Landish is a romance and cozy mystery author living in the UK, whose clean and sweet stories have tugged at readers' heartstrings across the pond and beyond. When she's not writing, Daisy spends her time reading, hiking at dawn, and riding into the sunset on her horse, Rosebud.

Join Daisy's Newsletter for updates and giveaways!
www.daisylandishromance.com

facebook.com/daisylandishromance
x.com/daisy_landish
instagram.com/beachesandtrailspublishing
amazon.com/author/daisylandish
bookbub.com/authors/daisy-landish
goodreads.com/Daisy_Landish

ALSO BY DAISY LANDISH

MURDER AT THE RETREAT

A MIKE AND MADDIE MYSTERY

PROLOGUE

Daniel Winters carefully placed the thick manilla envelope at the bottom of his suitcase. His hands shook no matter how often he told himself to calm down. This would be the make or break of his career, so long as he played his cards right.

He swallowed thick salvia and placed his meticulously folded clothes over the envelope. Once it was hidden, the palpitations of his heart slowed down.

Make or break. This was his best work yet, his *magnum opus*. From this singular manuscript, he was going to achieve all his dreams. That was if certain other people saw the same things he did. He had been working on this for years now, chipping away at the story bit by bit. The whole thing was rather nerve-wracking.

Taking a few deep breaths, Daniel headed into his bathroom. A low, dull pain started in the center of his chest, and he grimaced, reaching first for his heart meds—he'd forgotten to take them this morning—and then the Tums.

He took one first, then the other, and washed them with a glass of water. Finally, he grabbed one of the new pills the herbalist had given him. He leaned his head back and dropped it into the back of his throat before drinking. This was the worst one. It smelled like a rat and tasted like sticking his tongue into a battery.

"Damn heartburn," he grumbled, massaging his chest with a trembling hand.

With another deep breath, he grabbed his bag containing a toothbrush, toothpaste, and a fresh bottle of Tums. After packing them, he glanced lovingly at his old typewriter. Too bad it wouldn't fit into the suitcase. Computer it was.

Zipping the suitcase shut, he hefted it in one hand and headed out of his apartment.

Portland, Oregon, here I come! Hope you're ready for me.

CHAPTER 1

Madeleine Moreau took off her pale blue hat and placed it on the bed closest to the window. From here, she could see the Columbia River surrounded by the fragile green of fresh spring growth. Portland glittered in the afternoon sunshine. The hotels and apartment buildings lined the river, looking like little mountains.

"We've got a balcony," she said over her shoulder. "I want to wake up before dawn and sit out there wrapped up in a cozy blanket with a cup of coffee, watching the sunrise. We're even facing East, so it's possible."

Behind her, her writing partner and best friend chuckled. Mike was already putting his clothes in the bottom two drawers of the dresser on which the TV stood.

"You want to be outside before dawn?" he asked. "You, who are still wearing your winter coat?"

Maddie glanced down at herself. "This isn't a winter coat. It's a spring jacket."

"If you say so," Mike teased.

She rolled her eyes, grabbed her suitcase, and carried it to the dresser. Mike was finished putting his clothes away and headed out onto the balcony. As Maddie put away her clothes for the week that they'd be here, she couldn't stop a small stab of disappointment.

When Ben Hiddlestone, a fellow writer and Maddie's sort-of boyfriend (they went on dates but hadn't had the 'official' talk about what their relationship was), had brought up this writer's retreat, she had hoped that he'd be able to join her and Mike. Instead, he'd stayed home in Spokane. He told her and Mike to have fun.

Maddie had hoped that Ben would help her with this thriller mystery she had latched onto. Usually, she preferred things cozier. Ben was a well-known writer of mysterious thrillers, and Maddie had hoped to brainstorm with him.

Not to mention, she had planned to use this trip to figure out what their relationship was once and for all.

"Something wrong?" Mike asked her.

Maddie blinked and lifted her head. His brows were drawn together, a concerned frown on his face.

"Er…" Maddie shrugged. "I just wish we could have convinced Ben to come along."

Mike nodded. "Yeah, me too. It would have been awesome to have him. I guess he's got a point about only being able to write in solitude. But at least he, Trisha, and Carson have that hike planned. They won't be pining for our presence."

Maddie had to laugh at that.

Soon, her thoughts were turned to the retreat. They arrived a little later than they wanted and had to rush to prepare for the introduction luncheon. The retreat had only about twenty individuals participating this year so that everyone could sit at one table.

A middle-aged man with a thin, craggy face took the spot at the head of the table. He clinked his knife against his glass to get every-one's attention.

"Hello, everyone. Let's go around the table introducing ourselves, our writing backgrounds, and our aspirations," he said. "I'll go first. My name is Daniel Winters. I have published over twenty-seven true crime novels."

He grinned as he lifted his glass of water. His hand shook slightly, nearly making it spill.

"I'm currently working on an expose about a horrendous case twenty years ago. I'm here to gather the last few details before sending my manuscript to my publisher."

The next person in line, a red-faced woman with lank brown hair, flushed an even deeper red. "Um. I'm Denise Foster. I haven't published anything yet, and I'm hoping to get, um, feedback on my novel. It's a romance."

She ducked her head, clearly embarrassed.

Maddie listened with interest to every person. They all sounded so interesting! When it was Mike's turn, he grinned at them all.

"My name is Michael Malison or Mike. I've been working for a few years as a ghostwriter. I've done some indie publishing as well. I'm here to gain new insights into other people's writing processes and hopefully make a few new friends. I mostly write mysteries but don't say no to reading or writing any genre."

"I'm Maddie," Maddie said. She left off her last name for now. She folded her hands in her lap as she smiled around the table. "I work with Mike closely. I'm more of a plotter. I love to create an intricate structure for books, but I don't have the patience to slog through chapter by chapter to find the perfect words. I'm here because I have a thriller mystery that I'm determined to write all the way through, and I'm hoping that the ambiance will help me stay focused."

The man sitting next to her made a bit of a harrumphing noise. "I'm Percy Morris. I write literary fiction. I'm here because my wife walked out on me."

He tossed back his glass of what Maddie hoped was apple juice. It was certainly too early in the day for him to be getting drunk.

The retreat coordinator, Lexi Black, took over as everyone started being served lunch. Evenings would be reserved for making connections. Every night, there would also be a draw from an anonymous first chapter for everyone to critique.

"I hope that you all have a delightful visit here," Lexi said as she smiled at all of them. "It will be a fun, exciting retreat."

"If I wanted excitement, I'd have gone to Disneyland," Percy grumbled.

Lexi gave him a brief, frustrated look. Maddie had to wonder how much he'd been moaning and grumbling already. She hoped they wouldn't have to spend too much time listening to him.

As much as she could sympathize with someone whose world got turned upside down, she didn't think this was the best way to deal with it. Then again, she wasn't sure how to react if someone she loved walked out on her.

"I'm going to pass around a sign-up sheet for anyone who wants to be part of the outlining critique," Lexi said, handing a clipboard to Daniel. "This is for those who are just starting and need feedback on the story's structure. It won't be anonymous, so ensure you've got your elephant hide on!"

Maddie laughed softly. Even though she loved plotting, this was certainly something she wanted to sign up for.

She wasn't having an easy time hitting the beats she wanted. The pacing of her thriller seemed off... rushed and too slow at the same time. Some feedback would certainly be helpful!

"So, Percy," Daniel said as he passed the sign-up sheet to Denise, "what's a *literary* writer doing here? Come to tell us all that our writing is derisive and formulaic?"

Percy barked out a laugh. "Yes, yes. All literary writers are snobs who write pretentious, depressing pieces. I subscribe to the belief that there is value in every genre... and that literary is genre work itself and people who try to say otherwise are bloated in their egos."

Daniel guffawed.

"Let's not get into any of that," Lexi said quickly. She looked nervously at Percy and Daniel. "We're all here to improve our writing, right?"

Daniel snorted. He muttered something under his breath but luckily didn't push it.

Maddie sighed. Good. The last thing she wanted was for this luncheon to get sucked into a debate. There were so many beautiful things to talk about!

She took a bite of her food and watched the various interactions around the table with interest. There were so many diverse personalities here!

It would be easy to incorporate some of these people into side characters for her novel. Maybe that was what she was missing. A rich cast of colorful people drives the plot forward. Maybe she was stuck because she used the plot to drive her characters rather than vice versa.

"Denise, what's your romance about?" Mike asked.

The red-faced woman blinked owlishly at him; her expression startled. From how she was hunched in her chair, Maddie could see she was trying her best to disappear.

"Um. It's about this girl. Well, woman. She moves to a small town to care for her grandfather after he breaks his leg. And then she meets the local doctor who is a..." Denise glanced down the table as though searching for someone to interrupt her. "A, um... Werewolf."

"So, a paranormal romance?" Maddie asked. She grinned at Denise as she took a bite of her sandwich.

Denise nodded.

"Love it," Mike said enthusiastically. "I'd love to hear more. Maybe you, me, and Maddie can go hang out at the pool and talk about it more later?"

Denise gave him an uncertain smile, her eyes flickering to Maddie. "Um, maybe."

"Or we could find that fire pit and have a fire," Maddie suggested.

Denise nodded, looking like she was trying not to be too excited. Maddie smiled warmly; Denise was painfully shy.

The sound of coughing caught her attention. She turned, then jumped to her feet, seeing Daniel's face turn purple. He grabbed his throat, a wild look in his eyes. Lexi was the first to him, pulling him up so she could try to dislodge whatever he was choking on.

"Call the hotel manager," Percy yelped.

Maddie whipped out her phone, calling 9-1-1. An operator answered, and Maddie described what was happening as Lexi tried to help. Daniel slumped to the table. Mike rushed over to give his help, too. Denise pressed both her hands to her mouth, eyes wide.

By the time the paramedics arrived, it was too late. Maddie stood with Denise and Lexi, feeling shell-shocked, as the paramedics took the body out of the room.

Daniel Winters was dead.

CHAPTER 2

"It's just awful," Denise said. Her eyes were puffy and red, tears still trickling down her face.

Mike patted her shoulder, feeling that same weight on his chest. It wasn't every day you saw someone die right in front of you. He, Denise, and two other writers—Paul and Karla—were strolling along the path next to the Columbia River.

It was a beautiful, bright day. The freshness of spring filled the air with sweet scents, and birds sang mightily around them. None of them were paying much attention to it all. Denise had barely stopped crying.

"It's shocking, is what it is," Paul mumbled into his beard. His shoulders hunched. "I thought for sure he was choking. I thought he'd cough up whatever it was and be fine. I didn't even realize what was happening."

Mike turned to him. "I know. It's never easy to go through something like that. I'd urge you all to seek some trauma counselling. Because that is traumatic."

"Thank you," Denise said, sniffing. "I guess I should call my therapist. I live in town. I'll see if she'll have recommendations for everyone for the week at least... Guess I will not get any writing done anymore."

They arrived back at the hotel. The other three murmured to each other still. Karla said that there wasn't any point in just giving up on all the possibilities of the week and was encouraging Denise to at least try.

Mike only listened with half an ear. Several police cruisers were parked in front of the hotel. As they got inside, the other three split off toward the elevator.

"I'll catch up with you later," he told them.

Maddie's slim figure, dressed in an oversized sweater and thick tights, stood just outside the luncheon room where Daniel had died. Mike recognized by the hitch of her shoulders that she was watching something inside.

He trotted up to her. "What's happening?"

Maddie's expression was grim as she turned to him. "The medical examiner declared Daniel's death a murder. He didn't choke—he was poisoned."

Mike's shoulders tensed. Daniel had shown no signs of poisoning, at least not what he'd seen.

The detective walked over to them, a grim expression on his face. "I'm going to have to ask everyone in attendance to stay in Portland for the next few days."

Mike and Maddie nodded. They knew the drill.

"I'm going to have to ask you two to go back to your room now," the detective said. "Lexi Black will give me your information in case I need to contact you."

"Of course, Detective," Maddie said. "If we think of anything useful, we'll reach out to you at the precinct."

The detective eyed her but nodded. His expression didn't change, but somehow still grew more intense. Mike didn't like it. No doubt the detective thought it was weird that Maddie was hanging around like she had.

"Oh, there are a few things you should know before you look into us," he said. "You'll find that we've been involved in several murder cases in Spokane and one in Vancouver. But we weren't suspects. It's just that we were involved."

Maddie gave him a critical look. "You're allowed to say that the police asked us for help. We're good friends with Detective Carson Luttrell in Spokane."

Mike shook his head. "I didn't want to make it look like we were asking for an invitation into the investigation. That'd be weird."

"Oh." Maddie nodded. "Of course. We won't horn in; that's not how it works. Sorry. We'll just be going now if that's alright."

The detective hummed as he made a note in his notebook. "Please don't leave Portland."

His tone was dismissive. The two writers glanced at each other, shrugged, and headed for the elevator. Mike felt the weight of the detective's stare on the back of his neck. He tried to brush it off as they headed up to the room. Maddie folded her arms as she leaned against the side of the elevator, a pensive look on her face.

"What are you thinking?" Mike asked gently.

"That I thought was a murder. I'm trying to remember how everyone reacted. Lexi was the first person to think he was choking. Denise just sort of fell apart."

Mike shrugged. "Denise looks like she doesn't get out much. She seems like the kind to fall apart easily."

The elevator dinged open to their floor. They headed toward their room. Maddie was uncharacteristically quiet, that intense look still on her face. Mike touched her elbow, and she looked up, her gaze slightly unfocused.

"Hmm?" she asked.

"I think you might go through some trauma, too," Mike said, worried. "Let's see if we can find someone in town to discuss this. Normally, I'd say Carson, but I don't think it works so well over the telephone."

"I think we're all going to be going through some trauma," Maddie replied. "We saw someone die in front of us. But we're going to be fine. It's not like this is the first time something like this has happened. I just want to know why anyone would want to poison Daniel Winters."

Mike unlocked their room and held the door open for her.

Once inside, both kicked off their shoes and collapsed on their beds. Maddie had the one closer to the window, while Mike lay on the one closer to the bathroom. It was an unspoken agreement between them that this was what they always did when they shared a hotel room.

"I keep thinking about when he must have been poisoned," Maddie murmured. "It couldn't have been much before he died. For him to look like he was choking, it must have been in the meal we were eating."

"Unless he started choking because the poison kicked in."

"Are there any poisons that work like that?"

"I don't know, actually. I always use rare, quick-acting poisons in my stories."

They were quiet for a moment before Maddie rolled to her stomach and rested her chin on her hands. "Let's think about who had the opportunity."

Mike raised a brow at her. "We said we would not get involved?"

Maddie grinned at him, her eyes sparkling. "Oh, I don't mean to get involved. But all that writing advice is to write what you know, right? Well, this is the perfect setup for my thriller mystery. A small group of writers at a retreat, and one by one, they're getting picked off. Why? Of course, my story takes place on an island, so it's a closed circle."

"Are you sure you want to pretend this way?" Mike asked. "Don't you think it's a little insensitive to Daniel's death?"

"He wrote true crime. I looked him up while you were walking; he's the sort of guy who would start writing about the grisliest murders the day it happened. If it were any of us, he'd already start writing," Maddie advised.

"I suppose then he'd find it flattering."

"That's what I think."

Mike nodded. That made sense. "Denise was sitting on one side of him and Lexi on the other," he said.

"Ah, but Percy sat down after the drinks were poured and could have put something into Daniel's water," Maddie pointed out. "So there, we have three primary suspects. Lexi, Denise, and Percy. Daniel was being weirdly confrontational with Percy."

"Lexi is the one that set up the whole retreat," Mike said. "And Denise is just the sort of dark horse nobody would suspect. Her falling apart might just be an act. Or a guilty conscience."

Maddie grinned, clearly enjoying the challenge.

Mike shrugged off his concerns. Everyone dealt with trauma in different ways. Didn't he also like to turn fact into fiction so he could gain some distance from it? While working with Carson, they always went off into their spirals of plotting stories. The only difference now was that they had seen the crime take place.

Thinking of it that way, maybe he was the one that was being weird.

"What motive can they have, though?" he wondered aloud, trying to get into it. "Maybe Denise is his secret lover? And her romance book is about the two of them, and Daniel threatened to sue her?"

Maddie jumped to her feet, her eyes sparkling. "There's only one way to find out, isn't there? Let's go talk to her."

"What?" Mike rolled to a sitting position as Maddie rushed to where she'd left her shoes. "I thought we were still discussing the possibilities for your book."

"Yeah, but I need to get a better sense of who Denise is," Maddie argued. "You're the one who spent time with her after the luncheon. Let's see if we can pick apart what her novel actually is. She said it was a paranormal romance. I want to know more."

Mike lifted his hands. "What about Lexi? What could her motive be?"

Maddie hesitated, then took off her shoes again and returned to sit on her bed. "She's the one who organized the retreat. But we discovered it because of that newsletter in the ghostwriter's notice board. So, it was open to lots of people. She could have sent a direct invitation to Daniel. But then why…?"

"Maybe she's also a lover?"

Maddie wrinkled her nose, shaking her head. "No. No, she'd have to have a connection to one of the true crime stories he wrote. So, we should research the books he wrote and see what he submitted for the critique circles. See if any of that points to her."

"And that leaves Percy. His motive is obvious," Mike said with a grin. "He was insulted by Daniel at the luncheon, and it's a crime of passion."

"Or he meant to poison himself and accidentally got Daniel," Maddie pointed out. "Now. Who do we start with?"

CHAPTER 3

Maddie sipped at her tea, ankles tucked to one side under her armchair. She and Mike both sat across from Percy in his hotel room. They had decided that, since he was the least likely of all their suspects, it'd be best to start with him.

"I don't mind telling you, this whole death thing has unsettled me," Percy said. Unlike at the luncheon, he seemed sober now. "I tell you, I thought I would have time here to get out from under the shadow of my wife walking out on me. Now, it's like there's a whole unfamiliar shadow over me. Murder! Are you sure that detective said murder?"

Maddie nodded, keeping her expression neutral. "I'm afraid so. It was a mixture of hemlock and strychnine. Whoever did it certainly didn't want Daniel to survive."

Hemlock was common enough throughout Europe and the Mediterranean, but it had also been introduced into North America. It wasn't exactly tricky to find it, either.

Strychnine, on the other hand, was a compound that was processed from seeds of the *Stryphnos Nux-Vomica* tree. While the tree grew in India and Southeast Asia, the compound was used as a pesticide against small birds and rodents. Maddie didn't know any grocery store to carry it, but it couldn't be that difficult, either.

Percy's eyes widened. "Two poisons? Why would anyone want to do that? What do they do, anyway?"

"They're both alkaloids that act in the same ways," Mike replied, running a hand through his hair.

He'd worn 'casual' clothes for this interview. Meaning he looked like he belonged on the cover of a magazine. A dark blue sweater that hugged his torso and complimented his dark hair and eyes combined with a pair of black slacks. His expression was distracted, though.

"Both are paralytics," Maddie said. "And they target the respiratory system. That's why it looked like he was choking. His lungs had stopped working. The terrifying thing is if Lexi had given him mouth-to-mouth instead of trying to save him from choking, he might have pulled through."

Percy shuddered. "Any idea how long it takes to activate?"

"The hemlock takes anywhere between half an hour to several hours. Strychnine, when ingested, takes about fifteen minutes. So, it had to have been administered just when the meal started. The introductions took about fifteen minutes," Maddie said.

Percy shuddered again. "Then it must be that Lexi or Denise, doesn't it? They're the ones that were sitting right next to him."

"Did you see them touch his glass or food at all? Can you think of any reason they'd want him dead?" Maddie prompted.

"No," he replied.

"If you were to make up a reason?" she asked. "Like, maybe Denise and Lexi were both having affairs with him."

Percy gave her a startled look. "Why would you say that?"

She gave him a small smile. "Sorry. I'm sure the police will handle it, too. But the way I process trauma is to turn it into my fiction. I'm actually trying to approach this like I would a story. I'll never publish it, but I'm writing it into a story."

Mike's expression was frustrated, but she tried not to overthink that.

Percy shook his head slowly. "Well... I guess just before everyone else arrived, I saw Lexi talking with him. She seemed upset, and when I was refilling my drink, I heard her say something about it being not his story to share."

"Not his story," Maddie repeated softly under her breath. What did that mean? She could think of many things.

Now, though, she needed to get a lot sneakier with her questioning. Asking about other people was one thing. This? Something else entirely.

She nudged Mike's ankle with her toes, using the excuse to cross her legs the other way to do so.

"Do you mind if I use your bathroom?" Mike asked, standing.

"Go right ahead. There's a candle in there if you need it," Percy added.

Mike slipped into the bathroom, leaving Maddie and Percy alone.

She sighed heavily, putting on an air of sadness. Working under-cover was her favorite thing to do, and this was just an extension of that. "I'm sorry that I didn't get to know him better. I thought that as a true crime novelist, he could have done me a world of good."

"I wouldn't count on it," Percy said with a snort. "Trust me."

"Oh? Did you know him?"

Percy made a face as though he'd said more than he wanted. "We met before at a writer's retreat last year. I took my wife with me because she was writing a nice little cozy mystery. She thought the same thing. Maybe Daniel Winters would be useful to get some tips from."

"Did she cheat on you with him?" Maddie gasped, her eyes widening.

"What? No! Nothing of the sort. My wife, or ex-wife, whatever the case might be now, would never do that. She was never one to sneak around. She walked out on me, but that was because I was too stub-born to make a few simple changes… and it's too late now. She's been asking me for years to think more about her and…" Percy trailed off, his shoulders slumping.

Maddie studied him in silence. He seemed to be genuine. "I'm sorry. I didn't mean to jump to the worst conclusions."

"It's fine. Winters was a very… charismatic fellow. He stole my wife's manuscript. She let him have a copy, and next thing we know, he published it under one of his pen names." Percy grunted and shook his head.

"He had pen names?" Maddie asked in surprise.

"Sure did. He wrote under the names of Summer Daniels—not brilliant, I'll tell you that—as well as Danny Hunter. I looked into him a great deal, hoping to help my wife with her lawsuit against him. Look up *Moosejaw Murders* by Summer Daniels. That's my wife's writing, word for word."

"It must have been a tremendous shock to come to this retreat and see his face," Maddie said sympathetically.

Percy snorted. "It sure was! The bloke is lucky that I didn't get drunk enough to confront him. Did you hear that crack to me about literary fiction? It was like he was trying to turn all of you against me!"

"It was so unnecessary," Maddie agreed.

"He's lucky," Percy repeated. "If I'd gotten my hands on him, I'd have—"

He cut himself off, his eyes widening. Maddie tried to keep her expression neutral. He'd pushed too hard, and now she needed to ensure he didn't think she thought anything of it.

"Well, I'm sure that it'll be easier for your wife to get her due royalties now," Maddie said.

Percy stood. "Why would I care about her now? She walked out on me. I did all that work for her, and she just up and left."

Maddie thought about pointing out that just minutes ago, he was talking about how he'd seen it coming for years. But that seemed too cruel. Instead, she stood as well. "Of course. I'm not sure what I was thinking. Mike's been in that bathroom a long time—I better make sure he's okay."

Percy squinted at her, suspicion on his face.

She knocked on the bathroom door, and a few moments later, the toilet flushed. Mike came out, rubbing his stomach. He grimaced as though he was in pain.

"I'd stay out of there for a while if I were you," he said to Percy, then to Maddie. "I need to get back to the room."

Maddie nodded in sympathy. "Thank you for talking to us, Percy. Hopefully, the police take care of this ugly matter soon."

She and Mike headed out and toward their room. It was getting late in the day, almost supper time. They'd arranged to take their meal with Lexi but had about half an hour before they needed to get ready.

Once they were in their room, Mike shook his head. "He doesn't have any medications that I saw. Certainly, nothing that would have hemlock or strychnine in it."

"That was a long shot, anyway," Maddie said, crossing the room.

The view of the Columbia River looked especially beautiful from here. She watched as it lazily flowed through the city and tried to piece together what they had learned.

"Percy had the motive to kill Daniel if he was trying to win his wife back. I really believed him when he said it was too late. I think he recognizes where he went wrong and that the grand gestures aren't enough; his wife needed him a million different ways, and he disappointed her too often," she said.

"That's the feeling I got, too." Mike joined her. "I thought he was too open about everything he said to have been a killer. Even with your charms disarming him."

"Yeah, and why would he decide to kill the man when they still haven't exhausted their legal actions?" Maddie wondered aloud.

"It makes little sense," Mike agreed. "Besides, I was thinking about it more. Hemlock has an unpleasant smell to it, and both it and strychnine are bitter-tasting. Why didn't he smell it? Taste it? It can't have been in his water. It would have been too obvious."

Maddie scratched her head thoughtfully as she considered the problem. "He had that onion soup he was eating. It would have masked the scent and smell."

"Speaking of," Mike said, glancing at his watch, "we'd better come up with our plan for how we're going to tackle Lexi. Any ideas?"

Maddie laughed. "I certainly do!"

CHAPTER 4

The hotel restaurant was practically empty. No wonder, considering that it was earlier the same day that Daniel had been poisoned. Mike had to admit he had his own doubts. What if it was a random kitchen staff who'd poisoned his food?

Mike knew that the chances of that were so unlikely as to be nearly impossible. No, whoever killed Daniel Winters had been targeting him specifically and had been at the luncheon.

"I did everything I could," Lexi said, poking at her food.

She'd ordered mashed potatoes and a chicken breast; it was unlikely for poison to hide in there. It was why Mike had ordered off the kid's menu; the blander the food, the more likely he'd taste anything off about it. Maddie had ordered a decadent-smelling mushroom ravioli that was making Mike wish he'd ordered something tastier.

"You did," Maddie agreed with a nod. "Nobody could have known that he wasn't choking."

"But he was," Lexi said.

Mike raised his eyebrows. "The detective told us he was poisoned."

"He was. Oh, I'm getting mixed up." Lexi rubbed her forehead. "What I mean is, he was poisoned, but he was choking, too. I saw something go flying from his mouth right before he collapsed. I'm sure of it."

"Huh. So… the poison took effect at the same time as he choked?" Maddie wondered aloud. "Maybe he realized what was happening and tried to stop himself? And then that's all it took to weaken his lungs enough to make the poison kill him so quickly."

Lexi laid down her fork. "That's what the detective told me. I'm just so unsettled by all of this. I've known Daniel since I was a little girl."

"Oh? How did you meet?"

"My mother was murdered."

Mike winced. "Oh. I'm so sorry."

"It's alright. She wasn't ever really in my life. A socialite who was always drinking and partying. The cops never solved her case… nobody cared." A soft smile spread over Lexi's face. "Not until Daniel showed up, that is. You know, before he wrote true crime, he was the best investigative reporter there was."

"Yeah, I know," Maddie said with a nod. "I've been reading about him. He seemed like he was quite the colorful character."

"He was." Lexi laughed. "I begged him to come on this retreat. He was taking a vacation over in Greece and kept telling me there was no reason for him to return to the state. But he came."

Mike cut one of his chicken nuggets in half. He'd ordered plain water with his meal and was starting to really think twice about it all. There was lobster fettucine on the menu. And the wine list! He could have gotten the finest wine from Italy. Instead, it was like he was five years old on the family farm, eating the most boring food ever to exist.

Ah, well. He was complaining about the upset digestive system today. Tomorrow, he'd go all-out on the finery that was here.

"You know, he's the one that put me through university," Lexi continued. "He didn't have to, but he paid for all my classes. I never would have been able to get to where I am without him. And now he's gone. Poisoned! Just when…"

"Just when what?" Maddie asked.

Lexi shook her head. "Just when he was helping me with my debut novel."

"Percy told us he stole a novel to publish under a pen name," Maddie said. "I find it hard to believe."

Lexi clenched her fists on the table, her eyes fiery. "Percy is a drunk! Daniel Winters never stole a single word from someone else!"

"But he said—" Maddie started.

"Maddie," Mike said in a warning tone. He gave her a significant look. "You know what? I actually left my wallet up in the room. It's got my key card in it. Do you mind…?"

Maddie glanced at her ravioli and pushed it toward him. "Finish this; the hotel will charge it all to the room, anyway. I'm not feeling up to dinner after all. Just text me when you're heading up, and I'll be waiting to let you in."

She pushed away from the table and headed off, her shoulders slumped and head hanging low.

"I have to apologize to her," Mike said in a low voice. "She handles this sort of thing differently than most people. She meant nothing by it."

It was all going according to their plan. Of course, they hadn't known who would leave the table beforehand; they needed to know who Lexi would be more open to first.

"Maybe not, but it was very rude," Lexi muttered. "Daniel wouldn't have taken anybody's work and passed it off as his own. He wasn't that sort of person. He was kind. Why do you think he wrote true crime? Because he wanted to make sure those victims were never forgotten or written off."

"I never could read his work myself, but I've heard many good things."

"He was brilliant," Lexi said fervently. "And he still had so much to give. The saddest part of all of this is that the detective told me that the poison wouldn't have killed him if he hadn't choked. Oh, and because of his other medications. He could have finished his book."

Mike made a note of these details. What medications was Daniel on? What sort of medication would lead to the hemlock and strychnine killing him if the poison alone wasn't enough? Had the killer intended for him to take more, and he hadn't because he choked, or was it because the killer hadn't put enough in his food?

"This must be very difficult for you," he said. He put a hand on Lexi's. "Especially since you just had that fight."

Lexi looked startled. "Fight?"

"Someone heard you and him arguing about something... something being not his story to tell?" Mike shrugged and ducked his head like he was embarrassed. "I'm sorry—I shouldn't be listening to gossip and rumors!"

He sighed heavily as he speared a ravioli onto his fork and stuck it into his mouth. The sauce was thick and creamy, the flavor combinations making his chicken nuggets seem like dog food.

He could have wept at how wonderful it was.

"We did have a fight," Lexi whispered.

Right. He was trying to find out information—now was not the time to get lost in the beauty of food. "You did?"

Lexi nodded, looking ashamed of herself as tears collected in her eyelashes. "It was about his book. He let me read it... it was about me. Written from my perspective about my mom's murder."

"The expose he talked about."

"Yeah. There's so much detail in there that I told him about. I felt... violated. But he was trying to show a new angle to his work. How the crimes affect those left behind."

"But written as though it was you... that had to be raw and emotional," Mike said.

"It was stupid. I understand now what he was really doing." Lexi wiped her eyes, then pushed her food away. "I don't think I'm hungry."

Mike caught the server's eye and gestured them over. "Can we get to-go boxes, please?"

The server bobbed its head and left. They came back soon with the boxes, and Mike loaded up the food. Was there anything else he needed from Lexi?

"I hope you don't mind, but do you know what medications Daniel was on?" he asked, looking up. "It's just, I wonder if the poisoner knew."

"Heart medication and something for bronchitis, I think. He moved to Greece for his health. The climate agreed with him better," Lexi explained. She picked up her boxed leftovers and stood. "I'm sorry to leave so abruptly. I just want to be alone."

"Of course," Mike replied.

He gathered his own boxes but moved slower.

As soon as Lexi was out of sight, he ordered a second portion of the ravioli and a bottle of Riesling to be sent to the room, then headed back to Maddie.

She was on the computer when he got there, her expression intense.

"Daniel Winters suffered from heart problems and bronchitis," Mike said as he set the boxes of food down on the TV stand. "Apparently, it was a combination of choking, his medications, and the poison that killed him.

Maddie looked up. "What medications?"

"I don't know."

"Do you think we could get into his suite?" Maddie asked him.

Mike shook his head. "Not a chance."

"Hmmm. That's too bad."

He stuck the chicken nuggets into their mini fridge, and just a knock came on the door. He answered to find room service. They have him the second helping of ravioli and the bottle of wine he'd ordered. Mike thanked them, tipped them, and then brought them into the room.

Maddie shut her laptop. The two of them arranged a little space on an end table to eat at and sat down.

"Socrates was killed with hemlock," Maddie said as they ate. "But apparently, it was used for medicinal reasons, too. Some people use it to treat things like asthma."

Mike nodded. "There are a lot of poisons that, at the right dose, can be used as medication."

"It has nasty side effects even when it doesn't kill you, though."

"Like what?"

"Shaking. A burning sensation through your digestive tract, increased saliva, muscle pain, and weakness. Convulsions. Coma." Maddie shuddered. "If it weren't for the strychnine in there, too, I would have thought that the killer was actually trying to just make his life miserable."

It certainly would make it miserable.

"Did you learn anything about strychnine?" he asked.

"It might be what killed Alexander the Great."

Mike whistled. "Socrates on the one hand, Alexander the Great on the other. And he was in Greece. Wonder if it's a coincidence."

Maddie shrugged. "I don't think so. Pieces of this puzzle are missing... although I'll have you know, in my story, another of the writers has turned out missing. And they left behind a suicide note, but they're not dead... yet, at least."

"Really?" Mike asked, glad to be away from the macabre topic. "So, what's happening?"

Maddie grinned as she eagerly scooped up the food. "It started with the wine; you see..."

CHAPTER 5

Maddie sank into the hot water, sighing in contentment. She hadn't even realized just how much tension she had been carrying in her body until the heat relaxed her muscles. She closed her eyes, letting her head lean back against the rim.

"Thanks for convincing me to come down here," Denise said from across the hot tub, where she sat near Mike. "I was going crazy in my room, circling repeatedly in my thoughts. I know I'm being dramatic, but I just can't stop wondering if there was something I could have done."

"Like what?" Mike asked.

"I thought something smelled off after Daniel finished introducing himself, but I didn't want to interrupt anyone else."

Maddie opened her eyes again. She watched Denise's chin sink to her chest, her eyes following the tiny bubbles as they floated back and forth over the surface of the water.

"Smelled something off? Like what?" Mike prodded.

"It smelled… mousy," Denise gagged. "I thought maybe something was wrong in the kitchen."

Maddie straightened. "Hemlock is said to have a mousy scent to it. But if you smelled it, then Daniel would have had to have it as well. I can't imagine he wouldn't have, especially after putting it into his mouth."

A look of confusion crossed Denise's face. "Do you really think so?"

"Yeah. Did you see anything weird before he started to choke?" Maddie asked.

Denise thought hard, a frown on her face. Slowly, she shook her head. "I wasn't paying attention to him. I was trying to memorize what everyone else was talking about so I could hold a conversation with them all later."

"Lexi says she thinks she saw something come out of his mouth before he passed out," Mike said. "Did you see something, then?"

Denise shook her head, looking ill. "No. I didn't see anything. I'm sorry. Can we talk about something else?"

She was panting, a look similar to panic in her eyes. Maddie winced. It was clear this was not good for her. How could someone like this be a cold-blooded killer? It didn't seem possible. Denise was just… so worried.

Sure, some people might say it was a guilty conscience, but Maddie thought it looked more like an anxiety disorder. Her heart reached out to Denise, wanting to help her navigate these anxieties better. She had mentioned that she had a therapist, and Maddie hoped it would help.

"Let's talk about something else," Mike said.

"Yes. How about our writing? I can't remember what you two said you were writing," Denise said, looking relieved.

"I'm currently working on an epic fantasy for a client. I ghostwrite for the most part," Mike said. "Usually, I like to work on mysteries, but right now, I've got a change of pace. I can't go into a great deal of detail for it; I was hoping to get involved in the writerly atmosphere here."

"And I'm working on a thriller mystery. But I don't think you'll want to talk about it. The basis is very similar to what happened here," Maddie admitted. "So similar, I probably won't end up publishing it. So far, everything I've written has been more of a… well, self-therapy, I guess you could say."

Denise frowned at her. "Why would you do that? I write the world how I want it to be; I can't imagine writing something so bleak as how the world is."

Maddie shrugged. "It helps me cope. But like I said, it probably will never be published. Not in its current form, at least."

"Have you published before?" Denise asked, scrunching her nose.

"Only indie publishing. I'm privileged to come from a wealthy family. So my writing is more about me expressing myself and wanting to bring entertainment to the world, rather than as a serious career." Maddie waved her hand under the water, watching as the top rippled. "I love my work as a ghostwriting plotter, though. I've gotten a lot of good feedback on that."

Denise chewed her lip. "I'm not very good at plotting."

"Neither am I," Mike laughed. He pulled himself out of the hot tub and sat on the ledge. "That's why I do my best work with Maddie here. We're a good team. She loves the plotting. I love the writing."

"You both seem so… glamourous," Denise sighed. "I don't think I have the confidence to be successful. My husband always tells me I need to believe in myself more. But I just look at writers like Danielle Steel or Jane Austen, and I know I'm not good enough."

Maddie reached across the spa to take Denise's hand. "You know who else isn't Danielle Steel or Jane Austen?"

Denise gave her a puzzled look.

"Nora Roberts. Julia Quinn. And Danielle Steel isn't Tessa Dare. That's the point." Maddie gave her an encouraging smile. "You're your own author, which is much better than being anyone else. Now. Let's hear about this paranormal romance you're writing. Maybe we can give a few pointers."

"I don't enjoy talking about it," Denise mumbled.

Mike hummed. "Do you want to just go over some of the basic points for a plot, then?"

"Sure. Maybe that will help!" Denise laughed. "I know how it starts; I know how it ends. But how does it get from point A to point B?"

Point A to point B. Of course! Maddie gasped. She got out of the hot tub and raced to where she left her towel and hotel robe.

"What happened?" Denise cried, startled. "What's wrong?"

"Nothing! I just realized—how did the poison get onto the plate?" Maddie said. She hurriedly toweled off her legs. "You weren't aware of the smell until everyone was introducing themselves. After Daniel did.

The food was served first! So how did the poison get from point A to point B, the plate?"

Denise's eyes were wide and confused as she watched Maddie. "Uh…"

"Maddie. Slow down. Talk to me," Mike said. "What did you figure out?"

Maddie pulled on the robe. Her skin was still damp, and the cloth did that gross squirming thing that happened with clothes on skin that weren't dried off enough. She ignored it with some difficulty. She needed to return to Lexi's room before the writer's retreat coordinator went to bed.

"I'm not sure," she hedged in reply to Mike's question. "I just realized something. And if I'm right, then it's going to change everything. I just hope I am right! Because otherwise, there's a killer among us!"

She dashed off, ignoring the startled protests from behind her. Mike called for her to wait, but she didn't slow down.

In her head, she imagined this moment for the protagonist of her book. Of course, Emmaline Guthered wouldn't be running to get the last piece of the puzzle—she would have realized that the killer was almost on their next victim. Such a thing wasn't happening to Maddie.

There was only one person the killer had been after… and Maddie wasn't so certain that they'd been trying to kill Daniel Winters, either. Nothing made sense at first, but now she saw it all so clearly in her mind.

The elevators were on the tallest floor, so Maddie dove through the doors leading to the stairs. Her robe came undone and flapped on either side of her, her one-piece bathing suit leaving water droplets in her wake.

Her protagonist would wear a bikini. Bright pink with flower details at the waist. It wouldn't be on purpose—she would have thought she packed a different swimsuit, but the flowers would give her the last clue.

Yes, the hemlock would be the poison there, just as it was here.

Maddie shook her head, banishing the thoughts of her book. She was panting by the time she reached the third floor. As she stumbled into the hall, the elevator chimed. She glanced over to see the doors open. Mike and Denise, both wearing their own hotel robes, rushed out when they saw her.

Heat rushed to Maddie's cheeks. She tried to regulate her breathing as she waited for them to catch up.

"What is going on?" Mike demanded.

Maddie swallowed and padded down the hallway. She explained as quickly as she could. "The key is in Daniel Winters' expose about the murder of Lexi's mother. He wrote it from Lexi's point of view, remember?"

Mike nodded, looking lost.

A surge of triumph went through Maddie. Usually, it was Mike being dramatic and making her wait for the answers. But this time, she figured it out first.

"He might have written it from her perspective, but it's still ultimately going to be his words. His story," Maddie explained as they got to Lexi's door. She knocked firmly. "And with these charges of plagiarism coming against him, he had to make sure that Lexi wouldn't claim his work, either."

"I am so lost," Denise said, looking bewildered.

Mike nodded his agreement.

The door opened. Lexi was wearing a set of plaid pajamas, her hair loose. When she saw the three of them, her eyes widened. "What's going on?"

"Do you still have a copy of Daniel's expose?" Maddie asked.

"Well, yes," Lexi said, looking even more bewildered. "Why?"

"I need a copy. The key to his killer is in those pages, I'm sure of it."

Lexi opened the door wider. "All I have is physical proof. I'm not letting it out of my room, but you can read it."

Maddie nodded her thanks as she came in. "Let's get to it, then!"

CHAPTER 6

Detective Carson Luttrell smiled at his two young friends as they came to the climax of their story. He had to admit, he'd been engrossed in their retelling of the Daniel Winters case. He knew where they were going with this—he'd been contacted by Detective Beans in Portland about them—but Ben and Trisha were both on the edges of their seats.

"Oh, come on!" Ben groaned as Maddie took a long drink of water. "You can't just leave us hanging! What did you find?"

"First, it took us hours to read through that manuscript," Mike said. He swirled his cranberry juice in his wineglass, looking pensive. "It was worth it. So well written! It made me feel inadequate for sure."

Ben laughed. "Don't I know it! I read a bunch of Winters' stuff while I was researching my last book. The man could give Shakespeare a run for his money."

Trisha swatted his arm. "Noooo, don't distract them! Who was the killer?"

"In my book or in real life?" Maddie teased.

Trisha narrowed her eyes.

Maddie chuckled, then spread her hands. "It was in the pages of that manuscript we found our answers. Daniel Winters described himself as an odd, robust man who was too critical of doctors and put too much stock in new-age treatments. And that was how we got the answer."

Ben and Trisha both leaned forward. Carson took a long drink of his orange juice. It was nice that someone else could be the captive audience for a change. It would disappoint his young friends if he was the only one they could recount their dramatic tale to.

"What was the answer?" Ben breathed, his eyes not moving from Maddie's face.

"Daniel Winters killed himself."

Both Ben and Trisha audibly gasped. Trisha stared with a slack jaw while Ben's face twisted in concentration.

"He killed himself... because the only person who could put hemlock in his food was himself?" Ben asked slowly. "That's why the point A to point B discussion triggered something in your memory?"

Maddie nodded, smiling in a pleased sort of way. "Exactly. Only Lexi or Denise could have slipped something into his food while the rest of us weren't looking, but him? No. He'd have seen it."

"Not to mention he had to have smelled the hemlock before he ate anything," Mike added.

"Strychnine is odorless but, like Hemlock, has an extremely bitter taste," Maddie said. "Between the two of them, there's no way he would have missed it. So, it only leaves one answer. He introduced that poison himself and ate despite the smell and taste because he was expecting it."

"The detective found pills containing both hemlock and strychnine in his suitcase," Mike said.

Trisha leaned back in her chair, looking stunned. "He really killed himself. But why?"

"It wasn't on purpose. He was suffering from a weak heart and bronchitis," Maddie explained. "And while he was in Greece, he decided he didn't like the side effects of the medications his doctor prescribed him."

"He went online and started reading forums and sought an herbalist to give him the plants. He thought it would make him well again." Mike shook his head, sighing.

Carson shook his head as well. "It's a horrible way to go. A horrible thing for you all to witness, too."

Maddie tucked her long legs underneath herself, pulling her oversized sweater over her knees. "I noticed when he made his introduction, he was shaking. One symptom of hemlock poisoning is tremors."

"But how could he think that poisoning himself was a good way to cure himself?" Trisha asked, shaking her head.

"*Digitalis* is a heart medication derived from foxglove," Carson told her. "It's derived from foxglove, a deadly poison."

Maddie nodded. "Technically, the spice in things like chilis is a toxin, too. Historically, hemlock was used to treat respiratory illnesses, and strychnine was used to treat heart problems."

"So, what happened at the dinner, then? Why did it kill him if he'd been using it already?" Ben asked.

"The toxicology reports stated he had taken a double dose of his heart medications earlier that day. No doubt he'd forgotten that he already took it. Reading his manuscript, he portrayed himself as a much less likable character than Lexi thought of him," Maddie added.

Trisha frowned.

"The man in the book is self-aggrandizing," Maddie said. "But there was an undercurrent to it like he never truly believed in himself. Despite the success he had in his career, he didn't think he was all that great. It's clear he thought his reputation linked to that expose."

Carson drank more of his juice. "So, how does it link in with Percy's wife?"

Here, Mike chuckled. "She never shared her manuscript with her husband. She was secretly publishing under her own pen name, Summer Daniels. When Percy found out, she lied."

"She was building herself a nest egg to leave him. The whole thing was a lie," Maddie said.

"Wow."

Maddie nodded her agreement. "But with the lawsuit hanging over his head, Daniel was worried he'd end up in a similar situation with Lexi. So, he planned to slip himself a little hemlock. Just enough to make a scene at dinner so Lexi would feel badly toward him."

"That's what Maddie thinks," Mike interrupted. "I personally think he was planning on making overtures that Lexi was the one that poisoned him, so if she made a fuss about his manuscript, she would be viewed suspiciously."

"He cared about her, though."

"He cared more about himself."

Carson put his glass aside. "Now, that's not something either of you can say for sure. The man's dead, and whether it was malicious, a publicity stunt, or a simple mistake, we shouldn't dwell on it."

Both Mike and Maddie nodded.

They fell silent then; everyone lost in their own thoughts.

Eventually, Trisha stood. "Well, this has been very exciting. There's a lot to think about. But I've been here longer than I thought I would be. Copper is going to be worried about me."

Copper was Trisha's golden retriever.

"I'll walk you home," Mike volunteered, jumping to his feet. He gave Trisha a wide, flirtatious smile.

Carson hid his own smile. He was glad that their little circle had expanded. Having more close friends could only be a good thing—although the age difference between him and the others was becoming more and more obvious.

"I should head out, too. I have an early morning if I'm going to get these chapters written by my deadline," Ben said. He shook his head, clearly disappointed in himself. "Wish I could have been there with you."

Maddie grinned at him. "Next year."

The three headed out, and Maddie looked at Carson, lifting one of her perfectly groomed eyebrows.

"What?" he asked.

"Don't think I didn't see those faces you were making," Maddie said. "When did you figure out that Daniel Winters had accidentally killed himself?"

Carson laughed. "When Detective Beans called me and asked how much trouble he should expect from you and Mike?"

Maddie's jaw dropped. "He called you?"

"He certainly did! He had already figured out what had happened at that point. He just needed to wait for the toxicology report. But don't feel bad. Think about it this way: you didn't have nearly as much information as he did and followed your clues to the same conclusion."

Maddie wrinkled her nose. "I suppose."

"Not only that, but you have the perfect plot for your next book."

"You're right." Maddie leaned back into her chair, smirking. "It is the perfect plot. Now, all I have to do is write it. A spring writer's retreat, full of mystery and action."

"You could say," Carson said slowly, a sly grin crossing his face, "you need to *spring* into action!"

The End

BEST MAN DOWN

PROLOGUE

THE MYERS' RESIDENCE

Peter whistled as he checked through his suitcase, packed for his coming vacation. Everything was ready to go, and this was a vacation he was very ready to take. So much had happened here in Pine Grove the last few months that it made his head spin. Winter had finally settled in, making everything cold and blustering.

But that was just one perk of this trip. The weather in Florida was hot and balmy. Still Lake would provide plenty of recreational activities that weren't possible in New England at this time of year. He hadn't been this excited about a trip in years.

Sam whined from where he lay next to the empty fireplace, looking up at Peter with doleful eyes.

"Everything's fine, Sam," Peter told him. "Eugene will come and look after you while I'm gone. He'll take you on walks, and since he doesn't work, you'll be able to sit with him and watch TV all day. Won't that be nice?"

"Woof," said Sam, beating his tail once on the ground.

Peter smiled at his dog and crouched next to him. It was the first time since getting Sam that he'd be away for more than a few hours, and he had to admit he found himself quite nervous at the prospect. It reminded him of how jittery he was when his oldest was born and he had to return to work for the first time.

"I was much more of a wreck then," he told Sam, scratching behind his ears. "The wedding is only for a few days; I'll be back before you know it. Nothing to be nervous about."

Sam's nose wiggled, and he said, "Woof!"

"I know it's with Jessica. But that's not why you can't come. You wouldn't want to be cooped up in an airplane for hours just to be cooped up in a strange hotel room most of the time, right?" Peter stroked Sam's soft head. "I'm only going with her as a favor. Like friends do."

He could have sworn that Sam rolled his eyes at that moment.

"We're friends," Peter insisted. "And nothing more than friends."

"Woof," Sam said doubtfully.

Peter shook his head as he returned to his packing. Sam wasn't being doubtful. The dog didn't even understand what he was saying, let alone think there was something more between Peter and Jessica than friendship. They were friends... albeit friends who kissed sometimes.

But kissing didn't mean they weren't friends, right?

Being invited as her plus-one at a wedding certainly put more pressure on their relationship. Friendship. Peter cleared his throat as he closed his suitcase, satisfied that he had everything he would need.

"Friendship is a type of relationship," he told Sam. "And that's what we have—a friendship. A wonderful friendship, mind you. But it is a friendship. I will not wreck that. You wouldn't know, but I haven't been divorced for long. Melanie, my ex-wife, was an exceptional woman. It's not her fault we divorced. It's not mine, either. We just moved too fast, and then...."

Peter shook his head, his heart growing heavy as he thought of his ex-wife and his two adult children. Rina and Matt still needed to meet Jessica. He would have to have their opinions on her before he pursued anything. The last thing he wanted was to fall in love, only to drive a wedge between him and his children.

"I need to stop thinking," he told Sam, crouching to pet his head. "I'll be back before you know it. Be good for Eugene, okay?"

"Woof," Sam said.

Peter smiled. He picked up his suitcase and headed out the door. This was just the vacation he needed. All these questions about relationships and friendships would have to wait.

The Timms' Residence

Short and squat, Marconi loosened his belt, sighing as the pressure on his gut eased. He would pack even more weight if Aunt Verna kept feeding him so much good, rich food. He knew he ought to tell her enough was enough; he needed to watch what he ate, but it just felt too good to be looked after.

Besides, Aunt Verna wasn't the sort of woman you could say no to quickly.

The door of the Myers house swung shut as Peter left. Marconi watched the small image from the hidden camera in Peter's house. So, Myers was off to Still Lake for a wedding with Jessica Stern.

"Just friends, ha!" Marconi shook his head. "Maybe I should plan a fishing trip for this weekend."

CHAPTER 1
THE CESSNA

The twin-engine plane cruised through the air, the land beneath slowly turning from white and brown to greener fields. Every time Peter checked the external temperatures, it was warmer. He grinned, glad that the weather cooperated for this flight. It wasn't easy to tell in winter if he'd be able to get off the ground safely or not.

A few dark clouds were forming on the horizon, but nothing to be worried about.

It felt so right to have Jessica sitting in the copilot seat. She'd taken off her shoes, and now her feet were nestled in fuzzy slippers while she had one of those Snuggie blankets tucked in tight around her with her arms through the sleeves. Her eyes were alight with amazement even though they had been in the air for some time.

"I can't tell you how much I'm looking forward to this trip," Jessica told him as she glanced over at him. She grinned widely, her excitement palpable.

"Me, too," Peter said. They were at a cruising altitude, allowing him to spare some attention to Jessica. "I'm eager for fishing and hiking. No snow! I'm going to thaw out finally."

Jessica laughed, a sound that lightened Peter's heart. "Not going to lie; I'm going to miss the snow a little. But everything else makes up for it. Two days off work, far enough away that I can't be called in for an emergency. I'm not sure the last time I was this far from Pine Grove."

"Really? I thought you went to conferences regularly."

Jessica shrugged. "These days, they're all virtual. So, no need to leave my house."

"Well, then! I'll make it my mission to keep us both entertained and relaxed." Peter grinned.

She elbowed him. "Not too much, though. You're my ride home, remember... I don't want you to get so relaxed and thawed out that you decide not to fly me back."

The teasing glint in her eye made him want to kiss her. Peter allowed himself to fall into that fantasy for a moment, thinking about how soft her lips were and how right it felt when he was close to Jessica. It was so comfortable with her, and more than that. It made sense to him...

He cleared his throat and pushed those thoughts aside. Friends. He didn't want to ruin that. "Are you sure it's all right for me to be with you at your brother's wedding? People might get the wrong idea."

"Wrong idea?"

"You know. That things between us are more than they are?" Peter winced.

Jessica laughed. "That's the big-time lawyer eloquence, huh? But don't worry about it. I don't care what other people think... it's good to have a few rumors swirling around you from time to time, anyway. I just want a friend to keep me company."

"If you're sure," Peter said doubtfully.

"Why wouldn't I be?"

Peter double-checked Jessica's expression, not sure if she was still teasing or getting annoyed. Her eyebrows were drawn together as though she was confused. His shoulders relaxed slightly. At the end of his relationship with Melanie, everything appeared to be an argument. The two of them had somehow forgotten to communicate.

Sometimes, Peter was worried that his friendship with Jessica would end the same way, that it was his fault.

"I guess I'm just nervous," he finally said.

Jessica shook her head with a slight smile. "Don't worry. I'm not standing up at the wedding, and I doubt many people will be pumping me for information about my life. Honestly, I don't know my extended family that well. My baby brother wouldn't get married without inviting me, but he's always been the social butterfly, not me."

"So, you don't need a partner for it?"

"Nope."

"Then why invite me?"

Jessica rolled her eyes. "Peter. I will not know most of the people there. I want a friend around, so I don't get bored out of my mind. I'm inviting you along because you've been moaning about wanting to go fishing forever. I thought maybe I'd do something nice for you, too. Unless the storms chase the fish away."

Her brow furrowed with worry.

Peter turned back to the skies in front of them. The few wispy dark clouds he'd noticed rapidly gained more form, becoming thicker and darker. His hands clenched around the steering wheel. He should have been paying better attention… these weren't regular storm clouds.

His jaw tightened as he scanned the ground, hoping to find someplace to set the Cessna down safely. The plane shuddered, then jerked as a sudden crosswind hit them. He suddenly realized that the wind had been at their backs this time, blowing them toward the storm faster than he expected.

"Make sure your seatbelt is tight," he instructed Jessica, keeping his tone firm and calm. The last thing either of them needed in this situation was to panic. "This is going to be a bumpy ride."

CHAPTER 2
THE CESSNA

The plane bucked and thrashed, but Peter forced himself to remain calm, navigating through the storm. He had got above most of it, but the winds were still strong. Below them, all he could see were dark clouds. He kept the plane on course, though, focused on his job.

Jessica was silent in her seat, eyes closed and breathing deeply. Peter could sense her tension but couldn't spare any thoughts to soothing her.

Soon, they had passed the storm. It wasn't a large group of clouds, only a few miles long. Peter released a heavy breath. The wind was still something to contend with, but as he dipped the nose of the plane to get back to a lower elevation, even that eased.

"We're almost there," he promised Jessica.

She opened her eyes and let out a shuddering breath. Quickly, she pulled her pack from under her seat and grabbed her water bottle. "Does that happen often?"

Peter grimaced. "No. Sorry, that was my fault. I should have paid more attention. Looks like clear skies for the rest of the trip, though."

"Good," Jessica mumbled.

"Sorry," he said again.

Jessica didn't seem to hear him.

It was less than half an hour before they went through the storm when they landed. Clouds had started to form above them once more, and the runway was getting spotted with raindrops. The drizzle got heavier, and Peter was grateful they could touch down when they did.

Jessica sagged into her seat as Peter taxied to a stop, then laughed. "That was an adventure, wasn't it?"

Peter was surprised at how lightly she took their 'adventure.' "I suppose, yeah."

"Hopefully, the weather will be clear when we head home," Jessica continued as she moved off her Snuggie. "I missed seeing the scenery. It looks so cool from the air."

Peter smiled at her in appreciation, then turned the plane off. They got out and were almost instantly swarmed by a handful of people running across the tarmac. They greeted Jessica enthusiastically and bombarded her with questions as she attempted to introduce Peter.

Peter was getting overwhelmed by their friendliness when finally, they moved away. He used the excuse of needing to check over the plane before he joined them. It was the truth, of course, but after the harrowing flight, he also needed some time to decompress before being social.

The plane had sustained no noticeable damage. Peter did the after-flight check and cleanup, ensuring everything was in order. Once that was done, he unloaded his and Jessica's luggage. They each had a single suitcase, more than enough for a weekend. Secretly, Peter hoped this could end up being a little more than a weekend.

Although Jessica had her veterinary practice, she probably would not want to take any extra time.

Peter shook his head. He'd been keeping busy, but perhaps he should find another job. Retirement didn't seem to suit him all too well.

As he started toward the cars where Jessica's family waited, he spotted a person in the nearest hanger staring at him. When Peter turned his head to see him more clearly, the man turned quickly away. Embarrassed to be caught staring, or something more sinister?

Peter shook the thought off. He was getting paranoid. Nobody here knew him. It was a worker or something like that. There was no need to see shadows where there were none... he had enough troubles in Pine Grove with all the investigations he'd been taking up.

This was a vacation, and nothing was going to go wrong here.

CHAPTER 3
STILL LAKE RESORT

That night, Peter and Jessica were supposed to slip out and get dinner together, but just as he was about to head down to the car rental, Jessica knocked on his door. Her expression was twisted in regret as she gave him an apologetic smile.

"It appears I'm more of a central guest than I realized," she told him. "I've been invited to be part of the bachelorette party. I don't want to be rude to them… are you going to be okay on your own for dinner?"

Peter laughed. "Don't worry about it. I'm plenty capable of taking care of myself."

"You sure?" Jessica asked, grimacing.

Peter lowered his voice conspiratorially. "Are you looking for an excuse to skip the bachelorette party?"

Jessica considered the question for a moment before she shook her head sadly. "No. I'm kind of excited about it. I didn't want to abandon you after dragging you out here."

"You twisted my arm," Peter teased. "Pulling me away from all that cold snow to this beautiful climate… yep, you dragged me."

Jessica rolled her eyes.

"Go on and have fun," Peter urged. No, he didn't want to be alone tonight; he had been looking forward to taking Jessica to dinner. They usually just made food together at his place. It seemed like he would have to wait on that, though.

It's what friends do; he reminded himself. *And even romantic partners need to feel free to have fun on their own from time to time."*

Jessica hugged him. "I'll call around ten to see how you're doing. And if I need an excuse to leave the party, I'll talk about watermelons, okay?"

Peter snorted but nodded. "Sounds good. Have fun."

She waved as she skipped down the hallway toward her room. The bride's family owned this hotel resort and booked every single room for the wedding. It was a much larger affair than Peter had thought it would be.

Still, he was happy that Jessica knew so many guests. It gave him a chance to see her more outside of her element. In the vet's office, she was always calm and in control, and while it was just the two of them, she was relaxed and playful. When they had entered the chili cooking contest together, he'd seen a new, competitive side to her.

He hoped to learn more about her this weekend as well.

Since he now went out alone, Peter no longer wanted to go to the upscale restaurant he'd chosen previously. He changed out of the semi-formal attire he'd put on, switching to jeans and a t-shirt, and headed for a local bar within walking distance.

As soon as he got into the bar, he realized his mistake. The bride was having her bachelorette party in the hotel dining room—the bachelor party was here. And it was already in full swing, with the smell of beer and steaks penetrating the air.

"You made it!" a jovial voice cried.

Peter turned to see the groom, Michael, stumble toward him. A huge smile was plastered on his face as he slammed his hand into Peter's back in a welcoming gesture.

"I—excuse me," Peter said, trying to hide his confusion. "I didn't realize you were having your party here. I'll just—"

"Didn't you get an invitation?" Michael's face fell. "Cory! Cory, why didn't my big sister's guest get an invitation?"

The best man, sitting in a corner booth looking at his phone, glanced up. "Uh. Must have slipped my mind."

He turned back to his phone, a furrow on his brow.

Peter was distracted as Michael laughed and slapped his back again. "See there? You should have gotten an invitation. I want to get to know you better if you spend time with my big sister."

That was a good point. Come to think of it, that could very well be why Jessica invited him along. He needed to get to know her family as much as she needed to get to know his. Besides, these young men were all acting wild and drunk already. They needed a designated driver here.

It wasn't long after before the only woman in the bar appeared. She wore a short, body-hugging black skirt paired with a white shirt with a low-plunging neckline. Peter would have mistaken her for a server at the bar, except for the nine-inch heels she wore. The young men started whistling.

Michael, who was trying to tell Peter that he could shoot pool better while drunk than sober, didn't notice the woman. Peter frowned as she zeroed in on the groom. This wasn't the bride; he knew that.

The woman marched over. As Michael turned to see whom Peter was looking at, she grabbed him and started trying to kiss him. Peter jumped in as Michael cried out in protest. She yanked his shirt, trying to pull him closer. Peter pushed between the two of them.

"Leave us alone. Mikey and I have lots to talk about," the woman purred, flicking open the next button of her shirt. She wore a lacy red bra underneath.

Michael spluttered.

Peter opened his mouth, but before saying anything, Cory was there. He grabbed the woman's arm and dragged her toward the door.

"Hey," she cried.

"Michael isn't interested in you," Cory seethed at her, releasing her but still blocking her way. "You're not welcome here. Leave."

The young woman threw her head, her curly hair wafting around her. She put her hands on her hips as she lifted her lip in a sneer. "You'll regret this, Cory Atkins. All of you will regret this. You'll see. You'll get what's coming to you. It's only fair, given what you did!"

"LEAVE!" Cory howled, pointing at the door.

She rolled her eyes, stomped her foot, and headed out.

Peter turned back to Michael, who was rubbing his hand over his mouth as though trying to erase the kiss that hadn't happened. He looked angry, but when he met Peter's gaze, he tried to pull off a care-free grin.

"Back to the party," Michael cried into the silent bar.

A lot of cheering and drinking met this remark.

Peter shook his head as he slid into a booth, ready to have a moment aside. Kids. He was glad he wasn't caught up in this sort of drama anymore. But it seemed like Michael would not let this woman, whoever she was, upset him. He was already back to partying, attempting to shoot pool with a chopstick.

Peter chuckled. Ah, yes. He remembered those days.

CHAPTER 4
STILL LAKE RESORT

The following day, Peter woke up just before dawn. By the time ten rolled around the previous night, he and Jessica had been partied out. They used each other as an excuse to leave their respective festivities and then had some quiet time on Jessica's balcony playing Uno until they were ready for sleep.

Jessica wasn't an early riser, and so would meet Peter later. As for him, he knew that this would be the best time to get some peace out on the lake. He wanted to catch at least one fish on this trip.

Still, he paused when he crept past Jessica's door. The bachelor party events last night had drawn to the forefront all the memories he'd have of his own wedding decades ago. If his relationship with Jessica was going to develop into romance, it was something they needed to talk about.

He continued without knocking. While having a peaceful morning together would be an ideal time to have the relationship talk, it would not happen when she was still half-asleep.

Outside, a thick fog rose over the lake. It gave the air a damp, spooky feeling. Peter almost returned to his warm hotel room but headed for the docks instead. He'd come to fish, and it was far colder in New England than here!

Various row boats, canoes, and kayaks were pulled out of the water, resting upside down at the shoreline. Peter headed over there. As he picked out a beautiful rowboat, his foot knocked against something.

He looked down and gasped. A man lay half in the water. His face was pressed into the sand, barely out of the waves. His hair was dark and matted with blood. Peter quickly dropped to his knees. He cradled the man's neck with one hand as he turned him over to get him out of the water.

Peter stifled another gasp. It was Cory Atkins, the best man. His skin was cold to the touch, but he was still breathing, if barely. The frigid lake water continued to lap at the unconscious man's body.

"Cory, it's Peter Myers," he said, keeping his voice loud but calm. "I'm going to pull you out of the water."

Carefully, Peter looped his arms through Cory's and pulled him up the beach, just far enough so the water would no longer sap his warmth; then Peter stripped off his own jacket and laid it over the shivering man.

"I need help," he yelled toward the resort. "Help!"

CHAPTER 5

Jessica rubbed one hand over her eyes as she handed Michael a coffee. Everything was in disarray this morning since Peter had discovered Cory in the lake. The bride, Arista, had nearly broken down, and Michael was still trying to console her.

"Is there anything I can get for you?" Jessica asked the red-eyed blonde.

Arista shook her head, sniffing as she dabbed at her eyes. Either she had the world's best mascara, or her eyelashes naturally grew in that thick and dark. "Thank you, but I should stick with water. I just can't believe it. Cory was never the kind to overindulge like that. He hasn't gotten drunk once in the years I've known him."

"Cory can be pretty uptight," Michael chuckled nervously.

"I told you not to make him your best man," Arista said, her tone suddenly vicious. "I told you it wouldn't be any good."

Michael grit his teeth. "So, this is my fault?"

"No. I just meant—I don't know. I'm just worried for him."

Jessica cleared her throat. "If you don't need anything, I think I should find Peter."

Arista looked up at her with a surprised expression, like she had forgotten Jessica was there. "Oh. Of course. See to your guest."

Jessica nodded once, feeling awkward. Michael was clearly giving her a look that he wanted to talk with his bride alone, but as she stepped back, Arista's hand shot out and grabbed her sleeve.

"I just want to say thank you for being here. It means so much to Michael and me. I just wanted this to be perfect... and now for the best man to get so plastered that he fell into the lake?" She shook her head and dropped Jessica's sleeve. "I just don't get it."

"We were having fun last night," Michael said, rubbing Arista's arms.

Arista shook her head miserably and started sobbing again.

Jessica frowned. The paramedics hadn't been able to promise anything about Cory's condition, but he was alive when they took him to the hospital; his parents were waiting there with him while the rest of the wedding party remained at the resort.

However, Michael was giving her that look again. Jessica mumbled some appropriate sympathies and slipped away as Arista buried her face in Michael's shoulder.

She hadn't seen Peter in a while, but Jessica thought she knew where to find him. Her hunch was proven right when she headed for the lake to find him at the docks, taking pictures with his phone. She sighed internally.

One of the major reasons she wanted to bring him on this trip was to finally have the time and space to discuss what was between them. Every time she thought they were getting closer, it seemed like something else pushed between them. Now with this accident... she knew Peter. He wasn't going just to let it lie.

"Hey," she called when she got close enough.

Peter looked up. "Any word from the hospital?"

"Not yet." Jessica stopped next to him. "What are you looking for?"

Peter slid his phone into his pocket. "Just making sure I missed nothing. How well do you know Cory?"

Jessica got a twisting feeling in her stomach at the question. It was going to turn into an interrogation. "Not well. I'm twelve years older than Cory, and he was born just after our parents' divorce. I stayed with my dad mostly, and he stayed with my mom. We've never been close. I don't really know his friends."

"So, you don't know how long Michael and Cory knew each other?"

"Not really. I think they met in college?"

"Hmmm." Peter ran a hand through his hair, which he often did when brooding. "I overheard a few bridesmaids saying that they couldn't believe Cory would pull something like this. It seemed like they had little an opinion of him."

Jessica glanced at him uneasily. She didn't want to be the one spreading rumors, but she had something to add. "Uh... well, Arista was just saying something about knowing him for years and that he's not the kind to get blackout drunk."

Peter clucked his tongue as he gazed over the water.

"She also seemed to think it was a bad idea for Michael to have him as best man," Jessica continued reluctantly. "But I don't know what it's all about."

"When I left the bachelor party, things were still in full swing. What about the bachelorette party?"

Jessica grimaced. She didn't want to admit that she had felt like the chaperone to these women who were much younger than her. The conversation hadn't been to her liking, and neither had the plans. It appeared the only thing any of them wanted to do was get drunk.

"After the bride's parents cut off the alcohol at the resort, they decided to all get dressed in these outlandish costumes and go out to some swanky place for food and more drinks. They came back to the resort at about three, I think. They woke me up."

Peter nodded. "I heard some crying during the night."

"I checked on them to ensure they were all returning to their rooms. They were messy," Jessica admitted, wrinkling her nose. "I couldn't believe it."

"Messy?"

"Arista was so wasted she could hardly walk, and the rest weren't much better." She wrinkled her nose. "If I'm honest, I never really liked Arista's friends. She's a nice enough woman, but her friends are... off-putting. They seem to bring out the worst in her."

"I see. This isn't good."

How did she know he was going to say that? Jessica cupped her face in her hands, her heart sinking. "Why?"

Peter jerked her chin. "It looks like this is a criminal matter."

Jessica turned. Any leftover hope of a quiet weekend went straight out the window when she saw a police officer approaching.

CHAPTER 6
STILL LAKE RESORT

The police officer, Detective Cray, shooed Peter and Jessica back to the hotel until he was ready to talk to them. Peter wasn't happy with how quickly he dismissed them, especially as Peter had been the one to find Cory. He tried to give the detective some information, but Cray only told him more firmly to get back to the hotel.

Jessica was quiet as they walked back. Her expression was troubled, and understandably so.

Peter reached for her hand. "I'm sure it will be resolved in time for the wedding to proceed."

"Is that even a good idea?" Jessica murmured.

Peter had no answer. They entered the hotel lobby to find it empty. Everyone must have returned to their rooms. He ran a hand through his hair, and Jessica tugged him toward a couple of stuffed leather chairs to one side of the lobby.

"I guess we'll just wait until he wants to talk to us," Jessica murmured, subdued. Her shoulders slumped forward. "The last thing I wanted this weekend was another mystery to pop up."

"Yeah. I know."

Jessica chewed her lip. "I love that you are always figuring things out. You take a personal interest in people and try to help them solve their problems. I just don't like how often stuff has been happening."

"I can't control that."

"I know. And I don't want to ask you to ignore it when you see something that needs fixing." Jessica slumped in her chair. "Maybe I'm too tired for this conversation. My thoughts just keep going in circles. I just... it's like with my work. I get called off for emergencies that need me far more often than I'd like. But I'm not going to stop."

Peter took her hand in his, squeezing lightly. "I understand what you mean. Sometimes I wonder if I'm sane with these investigations I find myself part of."

Jessica gave him a strained smile. "Oh, you're sane. It's just your drive. You're a fixer."

The detective entered the lobby. Peter immediately stood to approach, but Cray waved him off. "When I'm ready."

He spoke to the desk clerk in a low voice, and the clerk made a few calls. Soon, Michael and his groomsmen were in the lobby, answering questions. Peter stayed where he was, watching Detective Cray work. He was slick, getting the groomsmen to divulge more information than they thought.

But they were hiding something. There was a caginess to their answers that Peter knew all too well.

When the detective dismissed the groomsmen, he finally turned to Peter. He strode over and offered a hand. "Mr. Myers. I'm sorry to keep you waiting for so long."

"It's all right," Peter said graciously. This was yet another tactic on the Detective's part. "What would you like to know?"

Cray glanced over his notepad, where he had been writing. "Hmmm. Well, you can start with anything the groomsmen may have missed. I understand you were at the bachelor party?"

How did he know that already? Nobody here had told him. Peter fought to keep the surprise off his face. "Yes, actually. A woman showed up at the party and accosted Michael, the groom. Cory kicked her out, and she said something along the lines of 'I'll make you pay for what you did.' I'm not sure if she was talking to Cory or Michael, though."

"Can you describe her?"

Peter did so.

"Ah! That's Kaia Lister," Cray chuckled. "Kaia's got quite the reputation around town. She's always making threats but doesn't have the gumption to go through with them. She likes to start trouble, not finish it."

Peter frowned at Cray. "What do you mean?"

"I mean, she's not the person I'm looking for." Cray grinned, his even white teeth flashing. "An itty-bitty thing like her working at the Roundhouse couldn't brain a man the size of Cory Atkins and throw him in the lake."

CHAPTER 7
STILL LAKE RESORT

Jessica found Michael at the hotel bar, nursing along a shot of whiskey. From his disheveled appearance, she knew he was still overcoming a hangover from the previous night. She had to shake her head as she approached. Everything seemed out of hand now.

The only thing she could think of was to fix this for her baby brother. And how better to do that than to aid Peter in his investigation? Right now, the wedding party didn't seem to think what happened to Cory was anything but an accident. She had to pick out more information before they figured it out.

"Hey," she greeted as she slid onto the stool next to him. "Where's Arista?"

"Hmm? Oh. Oh, her parents took her back to her room so she could calm down. They're insisting we keep going with the wedding as scheduled."

Jessica checked her watch discreetly. The wedding was supposed to be at five tonight. It was currently ten in the morning. She blew out a heavy breath.

"I can't believe they think we should get married while Cory's in the hospital. I don't even know if he will be okay yet, and they're expecting me to dress up and act like nothing is happening."

"I can talk to them," Jessica suggested. "I can't imagine they won't understand that you want to make sure that your best man is going to recover before you have your wedding."

Michael silently sipped his whiskey. There was a dark, brooding expression on his face that Jessica didn't like. How well did he really know his bride and her family? What sort of people would push ahead a party like this after what happened?

That would have to wait, though. She needed information about who would have it out for his best man.

"I can't remember when you and Cory met. It was in college, right?"

"Nah. Senior year of high school. I dated his sister for a while."

"His sister?" Jessica arched a brow. "And you two stayed friends even after you broke up?"

Michael gave her a pained look. "His sister moved to London for her schooling and ended things with me because I wouldn't go with her."

That sounded reasonable. They would have been so young, and Jessica believed nobody would give up their best education for romance. Not that she was going to say it.

"Cory was furious with her. They'd never really been close, and I guess that was the final straw... Cory went through a bad breakup at the same time, his girlfriend cheated on him, and I guess we just bonded as we got over it."

"Right. And how long has Arista known him?"

"I dunno, really. I know her parents and his parents go to the same church, and that's all." Michael frowned at his whiskey glass. "Though, come to think of it, I don't get what she was talking about earlier."

Jessica leaned in. "You mean he gets drunk a lot?"

"Drunk, no. He doesn't do that." Michael replied cagily.

"So, what does he do?"

"He has fun. He doesn't always know when to stop. He probably went down to the lake to swim and tripped." Michael tipped back his whiskey, grimaced, and set the shot glass down. "I better go get ready for the wedding."

"Michael—"

"Arista's right. I shouldn't have brought him. I should have known he'd bring... bad luck with him." Michael ducked his head and hurried away.

Jessica closed her eyes. Exhaustion played on her brain, but if there was one thing she took from this conversation, it was that Cory Atkins brought more than bad luck with him. The only question was, what sort of drugs had he got? And was he just a user, or was he a dealer, too?

I have to tell Peter.

CHAPTER 8

THE TROUT DINER AND DRIVE-THROUGH

The diner was packed with the lunch rush when Peter entered. Only one table was still open, and he took a seat. His gaze skimmed over the servers who were busy bustling from table to table. He soon found his target.

Kaia Lister was indeed petite. Without her insanely high heels, she would only reach Peter's shoulder. Today, rather than the vixen's outfit she had on from last night, she wore black slacks and a white blouse paired with a blue scarf around her neck to hide any cleavage that might be shown.

He waved her over.

The young woman smiled widely until she got a good look at him. Then she stopped dead, a panicked look coming to her eyes. "Uh… uh… what can I get for you?"

Peter glanced at the menu. "A coffee to start with. I'll need to look over the menu. Anything you suggest?"

"Well, the clam chowder is delicious. I have it every day." Kaia was struggling to keep a professional demeanor.

Good, she recognized him. This would make things a lot easier. Peter set the menu aside. "And what were you doing at Michael's bachelor party last night?"

Kaia's cheeks turned pink. "Nothing. I mean, it was my last-ditch attempt to win him back. But I was drunk; it didn't mean anything."

"I suppose we were all a little drunk," Peter said evenly. "You know that what you did, putting her hands on him without his consent, constitutes sexual assault, right?"

"How was that—" Kaia spluttered. "You're crazy."

"No, I'm a lawyer."

Kaia's face turned ashen. *"What?"*

People were staring, but Peter paid them no mind. He propped his elbows on the table. "You said you were there to win him back. But when you were leaving, you made some nasty threats toward him."

"I wasn't threatening Michael," Kaia protested.

"Ah, so it was Cory you were threatening?"

"Yes! I mean—no. I was drunk. I didn't mean it." She glanced around, her shoulders hunching inward. It was clear she would rather have been anywhere else but here. "Look, I know what Cory did. He won't get away with it again."

Peter narrowed his eyes at her. She didn't seem like a criminal mastermind, but he'd learned long ago that looks could be deceiving. "What exactly did Cory do that you needed to get revenge on him for?"

"Nothing."

"Kaia, the truth always comes out."

Kaia's nostrils flared. She glanced around again, but there was a gleam in her eye, almost as though she was secretly enjoying the attention. Odd. When she looked back at Peter, the look was gone. His eyes narrowed further. Was she putting on an act?

"Cory was a jerk, okay? He turned Michael against me. Sleeping with him was a mistake. He was messed up and deserved whatever happens to him."

Peter stood. "I don't think I will get anything, after all, Miss Lister." He pulled on his coat, but before he headed for the door, he looked her once more in the eye. "And something has already happened to him."

She showed no emotion. But did that mean she already knew, or she didn't care?

CHAPTER 9
STILL LAKE RESORT

ne O'clock

The wedding was supposed to be in four hours, not that Jessica thought it should be going ahead for any reason. She searched everywhere in the resort and saw no sign of Peter. She had a terrible feeling about all of this and needed to talk about Cory's habits with him so she could give Michael a reason to delay the wedding.

She didn't like that the bride's family was pushing hard for them to continue despite the circumstances. Anyone with empathy would just step back and allow the wedding party to breathe a little before continuing with such an important event.

"Wish I could just step in and tell them we're canceling for now," Jessica groused as she headed down to the lake.

Unfortunately, she already knew that would only push Michael into insisting the wedding take place. Despite their attempts to repair their relationship, he still pushed back against anything she told him.

To her relief, she found Peter was back at the scene where Cody had been found. He was standing ankle-deep in water, poking around the mud. Jessica took a moment to admire what a striking figure he made; his pants rolled up to his knees and an intense expression on his face.

He seemed to suddenly sense he was being watched, and his head jerked up. Relief crossed his features when he saw her approaching.

Only to fall into chagrin. "I should have told you where I was going."

"Probably," Jessica agreed as she kicked off her shoes and waded into the water. "What are we looking for?"

"We?"

"Yes. I want to find out what is going on, too. And I figure that since these mysteries are something you'll keep finding and solving, the best way to spend time with you during these cases is to help the investigation."

Peter seemed surprised at this, but he grinned all the same. "I'd love the help. So, I found the woman who tried to kiss Michael last night. Her name is Kaia, and apparently, she and Michael used to date. She claims Cory poisoned Michael against her and admitted she slept with Cory… not sure which came first, though."

Jessica processed that information. She waded deeper into the water, poking around for anything that looked out of place. "So, she cheated on Michael with Cory and then blamed Cory for it… nice girl."

"Or Cory turned Michael against her, then convinced her to sleep with him under the guise of revenge," Peter offered.

"I suppose." Jessica grimaced. "I think Cory's into drugs."

"Drugs?"

"Just some things Michael was saying and how he said it. I don't have any proof, but it makes sense based on some of the stuff I've seen from him in the past." Jessica paused and rubbed her eyes. She didn't like any of this, but if they were going to figure it out before the wedding, they had to share everything. "Detective Cray was back earlier. He assured everyone that it looked like a terrible accident."

Peter scowled. "And here I thought he would be sharper than Donnelly and the fools in Pine Grove."

"Yeah. I don't buy it, either. Could it be some sort of drug deal gone wrong?"

"Maybe. If we get the police to open their investigation again, we'll have to find something to bring to them, though."

"Like what?" Jessica asked.

She stepped forward, and a sharp pain stabbed into the heel of her foot. With a cry of shock and pain, she jumped back. Something stuck to her foot, and she toppled over in her attempts to balance on her toes to prevent it from driving further into her heel.

Peter caught her, scooping her out of the water. The thing popped off her foot and fell with a splash. Jessica saw a black triangular shape below the water.

"Wait!" she cried as Peter started wading toward the shore. "Get that before we lose it again."

Peter lowered her to the sand and waded back into the lake. Jessica checked her foot as he searched for the thing that stabbed her. No mark was left. She wiped the water from her heel and was relieved when the pain diminished. It hadn't punctured skin, at least.

"What is it?" she called out as Peter bent over.

He brought the triangular thing over to her. "It's the heel of a shoe. No telling how long it's been there, though."

"Wrong." Jessica took the heel from him. It was a high stiletto type that always seemed like a deadly weapon to her. "It wasn't that deep in the mud. It can't have gone in that long ago. Otherwise, it would have been pulled out or buried deeper."

Peter frowned. "Kaia was wearing heels last night."

Jessica grabbed her shoes and shoved her wet feet into them. Excitement pulsed through her veins. "We need to get back to the diner!"

CHAPTER 10
THE TROUT DINER AND DRIVE-THROUGH

Peter waited outside in the car for Jessica's signal. Kaia knew his face and would probably make up some story about him to avoid talking to him. She wouldn't know Jessica, though, and so she went in alone to do some recon.

To his surprise, the door opened, and Jessica strode out toward the car. He frowned as he watched her angry movements. Something had gone wrong.

Jessica slid into the passenger-side seat. "She's not there. I waited for a while but didn't see anyone who matched your description. So I pretended I was a new hire and snuck into the back to check their schedule. Her shift is over."

"Shoot," Peter grumbled. He rested his forehead against the steering wheel. What were they going to do now? His eyes shot open. "Detective Cray mentioned she worked at the Roundhouse."

"I know that place! Well, not personally, but Michael told me all about it. Let's go; I'll get the directions." Jessica pulled her phone from her pocket. "Michael said it's the best nightclub in town. Posh. Great music, great food, great booze, according to him. He told me he and Cory go there all the time."

Peter followed her directions as they made their way through the small resort town. His mind whirled, but he stopped making any assumptions; he needed just a bit more information.

"Same thing?" Jessica asked when they arrived. Her face was flushed with excitement, making her look even more beautiful. "I go in first, and you follow?"

"Yeah," Peter agreed.

She grinned and jumped out of the car. She wasn't dressed for nightclubbing, but Peter doubted the club would still be open for business this early in the day. He checked his watch—only an hour left until the wedding.

He grabbed his phone and called Detective Cray. "Cory Atkins had a head injury. What caused it?"

"What?" Cray asked, sounding cross.

"What caused his head injury?"

"The rocks. We found one with his blood on it. He tripped and fell."

"Thanks." Peter hung up even as Cray tried to demand what was going on. He hadn't heard about the evidence they found, so Peter wasn't eager to share this information now.

He headed in after Jessica. As he stepped inside, he saw a line of young women cleaning and prepping various areas of the club. They all wore tight, short black skirts, white shirts with plunging necklines that showed off a peek of red lace, and nine-inch heels.

What has Kaia said to him? About knowing something?

Jessica stood at the hostess's stand, arguing with the hostess. Peter joined them in time to hear the hostess insist that she couldn't divulge any of her employee's schedules.

"Kaia called out, though, didn't she?" Peter asked. "Because she needs to replace her heels."

The hostess opened her mouth and closed it quickly.

"Never mind about that," Peter continued. "Was there a bachelorette party here last night?"

Jessica gave him a puzzled look.

Trust me. Peter hoped she got the message.

The hostess snorted, putting her hands on her hips. "There certainly was. Because her family runs the resort, that stuck-up brat thinks she runs the world. Let me tell you, she might have rich parents, but that doesn't mean she's a class act. You should have seen her. Completely hammered after being here for less than half an hour. It was disgusting."

"And there were some groomsmen here, too, weren't there?"

The hostess's eyebrows furrowed. "How do you know that?"

"Thanks," Peter said. He turned on his heel.

Jessica followed quickly after him as he hurried back outside. "What is it? You figured something out, didn't you?"

"I have. But we have to move fast."

"We haven't found Kaia yet!"

"She wasn't the one who pushed Cory." Peter's heart hammered in his chest. "We don't have time—we have to stop the wedding."

CHAPTER 11
STILL LAKE RESORT

"What is going on?" Jessica asked, keeping her voice low as she and Peter hurried into the resort. He'd been so focused on the drive back that she hadn't dared ask for fear of breaking his concentration. "Do you know who pushed him?"

"I think I've got it figured out. I need just a little more. We need to find Arista."

"Arista?" Jessica thought about how she had been sobbing earlier in the day and how she and her parents were pushing hard for the wedding to continue. Her skin crawled—was her baby brother about to marry an attempted murderer? She clenched her fists as she guided Peter to the elevator. "I know which room she's in. Let's go."

Her toes tapped against the floor impatiently as the elevator made its way to the fourth floor. As soon as the doors dinged open, Jessica seized Peter's hand and pulled him down the hallway. They had less than forty-five minutes until the wedding. She wasn't about to let her brother marry some black widow! Possibilities rushed through her mind about what could happen if he did.

She knocked hard on Arista's door as soon as they arrived, panting with how quickly she'd run down the hallway. There were sounds of laughter on the other side, but they seemed subdued. She knocked louder.

Moments later, an angry-looking bridesmaid yanked the door open. "What? We're trying to get ready here."

"I need to talk to Arista," Jessica said.

"Why?"

She thought quickly. "I have a necklace my mother gave me when I married. I thought it would bring Arista and Michael luck if she would wear it down the aisle, or maybe she could have it as part of the bouquet or in her pocket. Just... I want to welcome her into the family."

Jessica smiled at the bridesmaid, whose angry expression softened.

The bridesmaid leaned against the doorframe. "Oh. That's sweet. Arista is getting ready with her mother down the hall. Room 426."

"Thanks."

Jessica turned on her heel. She brought her breathing under control again as she and Peter went to room 426. She inhaled deeply and put on a false smile as she knocked at the door.

The door opened to Arista's mother. Her expression was stiff as she looked Jessica up and down. "You aren't wearing that to the wedding, are you?"

"I'd like to talk to Arista, please," Jessica replied coolly. "I have something to give her."

"Arista is getting ready for her marriage."

A small voice spoke from behind her. "It's all right, Mother. I'd like to talk to Jessica."

She came to the doorway. Her dress was beautiful, with a creamy tone that complimented her dark hair. Her eyes were red from crying, though, which couldn't be hidden even with the contour makeup and perfectly curled hair.

Peter shut the door behind them as they entered.

When Arista saw him, her expression dropped. "You're that cop Jessica is dating, aren't you?"

"I'm not," Peter said.

Jessica felt a ridiculous surge of disappointment. She knew they weren't dating. They were friends. Good friends.

Peter continued. "I'm a lawyer. And you're going to need one. So, tell me… why did you try to kill Cory Atkins?"

CHAPTER 12
ROOM 426

Arista sank into a nearby chair, covering her face with her hands. Her mother harrumphed as she put an arm around her daughter.

"See here! You have no right to waltz in here and accuse my baby girl of something like that! What is wrong with you?" The mother trembled with rage as she glared first at Peter and then Jessica. "I should have known your family would be riff-raff but to sabotage your own brother's chances at happiness?"

She was very good at turning the situation back on them; Peter had to admit. But he had spent too much time in the courtroom to let such an obvious tactic phase him.

"On the contrary, I'm trying to help. You see, I have a pretty good idea of what happened already; I just need to fill in a few of the holes before I take this to Detective Cray." Peter was sure to keep his voice gentle. All the clues he had found pointed to more than what was obvious. "You said that they were all getting drunk last night, yes?"

Jessica nodded, a puzzled expression on her face.

"And when they returned to the hotel, Arista was so wasted she couldn't get to her room on her own." Peter folded his arms. "They weren't just drunk. They were high as well. Cory told you about

Roundhouse, didn't he? And when you went there with your party, he was waiting."

Arista started to cry. Her mother looked lost, opening and closing her mouth quickly. She made a strangled noise as she stepped toward the door, but Arista reached out and grabbed her hand.

"I'm going to get your father," Arista's mother said.

"I want you to stay," Arista rasped. Tears flooded down her face. "You're right. We went to Roundhouse. I was just looking to have fun. I've never done drugs, and when Cory offered me some last night, I didn't want to take any. I was already drunk enough, so I ordered mocktails. But…"

"But he slipped something in your drink. And since you were already drunk, your bridesmaids didn't notice." Peter felt the anger rising in him. If anyone had tried to do this to his daughter, he'd have killed them.

Arista chewed her lip. "I don't know. I didn't feel any different. It occurred to me that I should sober up. But I just seemed to lose more and more. I lost all my inhibitions when the groomsmen started making out with the bridesmaids…."

Jessica knelt beside her chair. "Cory pressed you to make out with him."

"He drugged her," Arista's mother snapped.

"I never was attracted to Cory. I thought he was kind of weird and socially inept, but I felt sorry for him since he never had any luck with girlfriends. He said that we should just have a friendly kiss. I agreed, but then he grabbed and shoved me into the wall." Arista closed her eyes.

Jessica grasped her hand as Peter moved a little closer, wanting to offer comfort.

"It's not your fault," Arista's mother said. "Honey, if Michael really is the man you think he is, he wouldn't care."

"Mother, just stop!" Arista jerked away from her mother, squeezing Jessica's hand tighter. "I'm so tired of your snide comments toward Michael. You've been pushing and pushing for this wedding not to be canceled despite everything. You're the one who told me not to tell him—I'm wondering why!"

Arista's mother huffed, and Peter moved to the side, blocking her path to the door. He kept his eyes on Arista, though. "So, Cory assaulted you."

"He didn't... he only kissed me," Arista protested.

Peter sighed. "Legally and morally, it's still assault."

"Well... that's all that happened. He pushed me against the wall and kissed me. One of the servers jumped in and pushed him off me. She started shouting at him, saying that he promised her Michael would want her back or something. I don't remember. She made us leave."

"And on the way back to the hotel, Cory sent you a picture of the kiss and told you to meet him at the lake," Peter continued.

Arista flinched. "How could you know that?"

"When I talked to Kaia—one of Michael's ex-girlfriends—she mentioned Cory turning Michael against her, and since Michael and Cory bonded in the first place because of a breakup, including Cory being cheated on, I realized he pushed that same narrative on his best friend." Peter shook his head in disgust. "Michael told Jessica that Cory knew how to have fun, but he wasn't engaged in the party. He wanted to stay sober for a reason."

"He told me to meet him at the lake," Arista whispered. "He said he'd show Michael the pictures and tell him I tried to seduce him. He said he wanted money, but... But I didn't go! I planned on telling Michael, but I passed out as soon as I got to my room."

"I know. Jessica told me she helped you to your room because you could hardly walk. You weren't in any state to attack Cory." He finally turned his gaze from Arista to her mother, his expression still calm and emotionless. "She wasn't, but what parent, upon learning that their child was drugged and being blackmailed, wouldn't want vengeance?"

Arista's mother stared coldly at him.

"Mother?" Arista's voice rose in pitch. "What... no. You didn't know."

"Except she did," Peter said, creeping forward. "You were looking for reasons to break them up because you didn't think Michael was good enough. Was it someone you hired to follow Arista, or did you plant spyware on her phone?"

Arista's mother shook her head. "I don't know what you're talking about."

"Detective Cray said what happened to Cory was an accident, that he found the bloody rock Cory must have hit his head on. But I found Cory face-down. The scene showed signs of a struggle, and the detective was too sharp to ignore evidence like the broken heel we found. There's no reason he shouldn't have found it, either."

"You're insane." Arista's mother fluttered, her head swiveling as though searching for an escape.

Peter continued to advance. He would have a lot of sympathy for this woman and her husband, except for one thing. "There's only one reason Cray would ignore the broken heel we found in the lake because he planted it. You planned first to pin the attack on Kaia, didn't you?"

"I didn't—"

"You paid Cory to convince Kaia to try and seduce Michael, so you could have a reason to break up the marriage. When that didn't work, you realized if you could get the detective to interrupt the wedding and accuse Michael of murder… well, that was even better."

Arista sagged against Jessica, her eyes wide with betrayal. "Mother?"

"I… I… he's not right for you!" the mother exploded. Then she slapped both hands to her mouth.

Peter let out a heavy breath. So, the truth was out. He pulled his phone from his pocket. Time to call his contact in the FBI, Tiff. She'd ensure a proper investigation was done—into Arista's parents and the corrupt Detective Cray.

EPILOGUE
THE CESSNA

"So, when Kaia said she knew what happened, she was referring to Cory drugging Arista," Jessica said.

It had been a very intense, confusing last few hours on their so-called vacation, and she was more than ready to return to life's daily chaos. She was bundled up in a fuzzy blanket as Peter drove back toward Pine Grove through clear skies.

"Yeah," Peter agreed. "Though I don't know if she planned to tell Michael or not. I think she thought she still had a chance with him still... and apparently, she cheated on him with several men before Cory met her at a party. She didn't know he and Michael were friends but...."

Jessica shook her head. Her brother certainly had a dramatic love life. "I'm just glad he and Arista have agreed to go to couple's counseling about this and not rush into getting married."

Peter nodded once. "It's a good call. And I'm glad that Cory is going to recover. He deserves the trial that's coming to him."

Jessica nodded in agreement.

The unfortunate thing about this was that she never got to ask Peter where he was in their relationship. Now it just seemed a little silly. She sighed heavily, resting her head against the window.

"Penny for your thoughts?" Peter asked.

"I just... don't know why love has to be so hard."

Peter was silent for a moment and then murmured, "It doesn't have to be."

"It doesn't? Look at what happened at this wedding. Isn't this what happened to you and Melanie? To Henry and me? Love is hard. Sometimes, it's too hard."

"I disagree. Love is simple. The hard part is life. Really knowing each other, staying in love even when you see the other person's faults." Peter hummed as he watched the clouds pensively. "If two people know what they want, and they know themselves, then it's easier. They can be open and honest with what they want."

Jessica's heart skipped a beat. "Well... what if I know what I want?"

Peter smiled at her, his eyes sparkling. "Then tell me."

Timms Residence

Marconi dumped the hanger overalls in the corner of his room and gently nudged a cat out of his way. That had been a far more dramatic trip than he'd intended. Peter had figured out the mystery himself on the plus side, and Marconi hadn't had to reveal his presence. He was still impressed with the swing that old woman took when she brained the guy on the docks.

If he hadn't been watching to pull the man out of the water, Peter would have investigated a murder.

Aunt Verna hummed as she entered the room, carrying the giant sandwich Marconi had just told her he wasn't hungry for. "Are you taking care of yourself and staying out of trouble?"

Marconi sighed as he took the sandwich. Better to capitulate. "I am. And I'm keeping Peter out of trouble, too."

Aunt Verna smiled and patted the top of his head. "Good boy. Make sure you keep it that way."

The End

THE CASE OF THE MISSING MILLIONS

AN ANNIE ARCHER PARANORMAL COZY MYSTERY

PROLOGUE

Steven Langdon pulled on the sleeves of his sport coat and tried to exude confidence as he walked across the bar. That was what he called 'the long walk' as though this was a set path he had to take. In a sense, it was. How else would he reach the pretty girl perched on the barstool opposite the mirror, just waiting for the right guy to make the right move? He knew this for a fact, for he could see how she watched the room in her reflection.

Realistically, Steven wasn't expecting much, even if he put his best strut into play: holding his shoulders back, gut sucked in as he made this particular trek. The long walk ended with rejection more often than not. But it was better than staying home with frozen dinners and reruns. And occasionally, it yielded results.

This woman was way out of his league, even if he was sure she had winked at him. Maybe he was wrong, perhaps she had something else in mind or was looking at someone else, but if there were even a chance with her…well, he'd be a fool not to take it.

So, he strolled over with a well-practiced charming smile and stood next to where she was sitting. She'd turned to watch him approach, her back was to the bar, and her long, shapely legs were on display. She wore a short-back dress, and a necklace glittered in the neon lights surrounding the bar, glittering and expensive. Her hair cascaded down her back in waves giving her a sophisticated look at odds with her pixie face and upturned lips, which hinted at sin and mischief.

She watched him from the corner of her eye, and when she did not object to his presence, he took a chance and slung one leg over the stool next to her. If anything, she seemed to smile a bit more as he sat.

Good God in heaven. She was actually smiling right at him.

She twisted on her perch so she was looking directly at him, and her lips curled into a smoldering grin that sent electricity sparking down his spine. "You certainly took your time getting here."

He was at a loss for words. Not only had she indeed winked at him, but she'd waited for him. And he had kept her waiting. He kicked himself for that, at the same time, not believing his luck. While trying to find an appropriate response, he stalled by waving down the barkeep and he ordered another round for them both.

"I wanted to know there wasn't another rooster on the porch."

Okay, maybe not the best opening line, but his mother had always said to be himself. And this was about as real as it got. Maybe it was better in some ways to get these awkward fumbling lines out of the way right out the gate, so they could focus on getting right to the point.

She looked at him for a long moment and then burst into laughter. It was a throaty, deep laugh. He mentally kicked himself, thinking this whole game was over before it started. He made a movement to turn away, anger kindling in the pit of his belly though it was hard to say whether it was directed at her or himself.

"Wait, you." She turned further to retrieve her new drink from the bar, and her knees touched his. She seemed unaware of the contact or at least unconcerned. Or maybe…it was deliberate? She hadn't been put off, even if she'd seemed amused.

Steven drank his beer almost desperately as she made inroads into her margarita. From the glasses around the bar, he couldn't tell if it was her second or third, but if it had been more than that, she would have been showing more signs of drunkenness. Or she could really hold her liquor. He wasn't sure what he thought about that. His mother had also told him nice girls didn't drink, and so far, his mother had been right once tonight. This new detail added a hint of uneasiness. Of dislike.

Only the woman was talking, introducing herself as Carla Mendes, and offering her hand. Ladylike in accepting the pressure of his fingers against hers. Maybe his mother was wrong about some things.

He relaxed, settling into the conversation. This proved disappointing, too, for other than her name, she wasn't too forthcoming with information about herself. The conversation returned to him as if she found him fascinating when he pressed.

As she faced the bottom of the empty glass, he hesitated. She wasn't drunk, but another would likely push that over the edge. On the other hand, if he didn't buy another round, he would look cheap. He wasn't used to ladies who were this fancy.

The decision, ultimately, was taken out of his hands. "Hey," she laid a hand on his thigh and squeezed it. "I have an idea; let's continue this conversation someplace...quieter."

Steven smiled, thinking how nicely that settled things, and stroked her arm to convey just how much he liked the idea. "I like the sound of that. What did you have in mind?"

"I've got a hotel," Carla waved off the details as though they were insignificant. "How about we go back there? I might even have an extra bottle somewhere we can tap into." Her hand slid up his thigh, and Steven knew that he would agree to nearly anything this beauty would ask of him. "You drive," she added, "I'm not sure I should."

Steven jumped off the barstool, thinking that if this was the way his luck was going, he should buy lottery tickets. Carla was incredible. She could have been a model or a beauty contestant. Something. Something well out of his reach. And here she was, asking him to go to her hotel.

He settled the final bill at the bar with a shaking hand and offered his arm to Carla. She gave him a curious look and took his elbow, smiling.

The warmth rose from the tar of the parking lot, despite the cool of the evening. She grabbed his arm tighter, partially because she wasn't very steady on her high heels.

"This is your car?" She let a low whistle express her appreciation for the ride. "Nice."

Was it? He looked at his car, an ordinary grey sedan, and wondered. He kept it nice, sure, but it wasn't anything special. Though who was he to argue? Maybe this Carla liked sedans. Or Toyotas. Did it matter?

Steven palmed open the door and handed her in like a lady climbing into a carriage. The interior of his car nicely framed her long legs, and if her skirt rose slightly, she didn't seem too concerned.

He nearly sprinted over to the driver's side and slid into the car beside her. "Where to?"

"I can't remember the name," she shook her head, "but I can lead you there. Just turn right out of the parking lot and go about a mile."

She pointed to another left, another right, and two more lefts until Steven felt slightly uncomfortable. This wasn't taking him to the finer points in town as he'd expected. Downtown, on the Square, there was a rather lovely place. She seemed to be heading them out toward the highway.

"That's far from where we met."

"Yeah," she crossed her legs and seemed to settle in the seat like a cat with a bowl of cream. "I wanted to get out, and someone told me that was the best place for bars. They were right about that much." Her hand rested on his inner thigh. "I found you there, didn't I?"

There was indeed a hotel at the end of her directions. It wasn't… horrible…exactly, but it was much less expensive than he expected. She had seemed so…classy at the bar.

His face tightened. Pretty dress and fancy necklaces aside, he was starting to feel lied to. His mother had warned him about that too. Women who made themselves out to be someone they were not. Girls like that needed to be taken down a peg.

He parked the car and came around to get her door, thinking he would have to have a few choice words with her once they got inside.

CHAPTER 1

*"9*11, *what is your emergency?"*

"HE'S GOING TO KILL ME!" The woman screamed into the phone. Where was she? The room felt sterile. A hotel? The morning sun broke through the curtains, and the woman shrunk back from the light. Her face was flushed as though from exertion. "HE'S GOING TO KILL ME!"

She paced in the shadows, darting glances over her shoulder as though something was behind her. No. Someone behind her. Where?

"Ma'am, who...who's going to kill..."

"He's mad! He's mad!"

The woman gave an ear-piercing howl and staggered back. The phone tumbled to the floor, the screen shattering under the heel of a boot. Everything went dark.

Annie Archer shot upright in bed, her breath coming in short gasps. She had been dreaming again. It was always a certain kind of dream which woke her like this, heart racing, unable to breathe. No. Not dreams. Visions.

You're not there. You're not her.

It took a minute. It always did. She was grounding herself, finding reality. She could feel the concern from her roommate, hovering silently across the room. Ghosts were not great on sympathy, however. For them, the worst had already happened. Her distress was more a curiosity than something to be concerned over.

She waved Monty off. Let the ghost find something else to puzzle over.

Why had her mind brought her to the same place all over again? Who the woman was or where she didn't know. Once again, it ended before whoever or whatever came through the door. Or was someone already in the room? She probed her mind for answers even as she tried to breathe slowly again. It wasn't there. That it was a "true dream" was undeniable. She'd had them long enough, often enough to tell the difference; whomever this woman was, her life was in grave danger. Or soon would be.

Annie lay back against the mattress, her pillowcase was soaked with sweat, and the sheets were hopelessly twisted around her. The light from the window filtered the darkness of her bedroom, and the reassuring sounds of sleepy birdsong and the world coming back to life faintly slipped into the room. It would soon be dawn and time to start the day.

There was no point in trying to go back to sleep. Not now. The same dream had come to her three times in three nights and demanded she do something about it. What exactly was somewhat less clear?

The lurid red numbers on the nightstand informed her that it was currently 4:48 am. She told herself she would have to be up in an hour or two anyway, and just now, she needed to refresh herself, get the image contained so it could be studied. Even her friend and occasional partner, Sheriff Adam Parker could do nothing without a clearer vision. What hotel? Was it something local or somewhere else entirely? What woman? Who was going to kill her?

She grabbed the notebook and pen beside the bed and switched on the light. She jotted down everything she could remember this time. The previous two entries focused on the woman, this time; she could look around the room, at least a little—no convenient signs stating the hotel's name. No "HELLO MY NAME IS" tag on her clothing to help there, either. But the room was neither luxurious, nor someplace that would rent by the hour. Mid-level accommodations. Her dress was nicely made but not expensive. The phone, however, was state-of-the-art brand new. Her purse… here Annie's fading images betrayed her. Something important teased at her memory, just out of reach. What was it?

It was gone. She could feel it there, stuck somewhere in the dimmest recesses of her brain, but when she probed at it, she found only a hollow, like a tongue seeking out an extracted tooth.

Nothing.

Her eyes drifted shut as she thought. It was too early to be up. She was floating, sleep teasing at the edges of her consciousness.

Only for a minute. A little more sleep before I start the day.

Her vision from before rewound. Started from the beginning. The woman. The hotel room. Wait. No. She was drifting further back to a bar. She saw someone she knew seated at another table. A woman she'd met at some function or another.

Real. These were real people, then. Somewhere nearby. Here the woman wasn't screaming. She was nursing a drink at the bar. Alone. Their eyes fastened on the mirror opposite her. No. She was watching the room behind her and looking for something without wanting to be noticed for looking until something caught her eye.

Annie strained, trying to see. Attempting to direct the vision but lucid dreaming techniques didn't work well on visions. The scene shifted. Back to the hotel room. The phone call. Everything was as it was before.

The call.

The cracked screen.

Everything is going dark.

Dark.

Her mind drifted. Slipped over into true dreaming until…

The alarm went off.

Annie's eyes shot open. One hand came up to push at her phone, trying to make the alarm stop. It kind of worked. The phone dropped on the floor next to the bed.

The phone dropping to the floor.

Annie started sweating. Triggered.

It's not real. It's not my phone. It is my phone, but the one I'm thinking of isn't. My phone isn't broken. It's fine.

Her hand shaking, Annie reached under the bed, fishing around until she found her phone, relieved to see the screen intact, the snooze alarm informing her she had seven more minutes of slumber.

She grimaced and sat up, wiping the sweat on her face with the edge of the sheet. The last thing she wanted was sleep.

"I need to call Adam." She spoke aloud, testing her voice in the empty room. The notepad next to the bed confirmed this. Three dreams. Four if you counted the fragment she had just had. Was it too early to wake him? She wasn't sure what shift he was on. He'd said he was working late, taking some nights on duty to relieve another man whose wife was in the hospital. Was last night one of those nights? If so, he'd have gotten off a couple of hours ago and was probably asleep.

He wouldn't mind. Annie flushed, thinking of the closeness which had developed between herself and the handsome Sheriff. Especially if she told him what she'd been dreaming. The short burst of the scene in the bar had told her she was seeing something real. The more she thought about it, the more she was sure she'd recognized a few faces in the crowd. These people lived in or around Turtle Bay, the town she called home. She wasn't chasing ghosts or fantasies; the woman who was screaming was as real as the rest.

It might not be too late to save her.

CHAPTER 2

What she needed was a potion.

Annie Archer was many things. Sure, she worked in security and had a good relationship with local law enforcement, to the point where she did consulting work from time to time with them. She also considered herself to be a pretty good friend. Not to mention she had a…well, a thing of some sort with Adam, which might be regarded as more than a friendship, even if they were taking things quickly. Casual. With benefits.

She was also a witch.

Of course, this was not to be confused with Halloween stories of evil witches who lived in gingerbread houses and ate children. She considered herself a pretty good witch who focused on good deeds. She liked finding ways to help those in her community through her potions. She wasn't above casting the occasional spell to ensure good weather for essential things like track and field day at the elementary school or the church picnic.

It was her witchcraft she needed to call on now if she was going to convince Adam, as Sheriff, to look into things officially. She simply needed more details than she had from her visions. She required a combination of self-hypnosis and perhaps a dab of something to enhance her memory and give her a clearer view of what had happened.

"It's perfectly safe," she informed Monty as if he cared. He didn't. He was stalking the neighbor's cat in the garden where she was picking herbs. The cat, unlike more humans, had no problem seeing the ghost and arched its back, hissing, tail exploding to three times its standard size.

She ignored them and concentrated on the ingredients she'd gathered thus far. Memory enhancer was perfectly safe as a spell. Tricky though. Too much, and you'd be remembering every single detail of your life for the next week, right down to how your shoes pinched your toes while you were shopping to the feel of the couch cushion under your hand when you'd been looking for the remote. An overload of detail was no picnic.

But neither was dying, so maybe it was worth the inconvenience if she could save some woman's life.

Satisfied she had what she needed, she headed back into the house to prepare the potion. It didn't take long and could be ingested in tea, which would help disguise the bitter taste. While she waited for it to steep, she considered calling Adam.

No. Only when she had more answers.

Finally, tea in hand, she settled somewhere quiet and prepared herself to explore the visions again. Self-hypnosis was a new idea, brought up lately by a witch she knew well and respected greatly. She'd suggested that the hypnotic state shared many similarities to the sleep state where visions were usually seen. By putting oneself into the hypnotic state, you can retain information better and have more control over directing the vision.

Annie drank her tea and sat back to wait for the potion to take effect.

I hope this works.

⁂

Adam wasn't the happiest at being woken up. Annie had been right about him working late and going to bed not long after getting home.

She chastised herself for not remembering such a simple detail why he'd told her that specifically last Thursday at 8:11 pm when they'd been waiting for the popcorn to finish popping before sitting down to watch a movie.

Annie blinked. Wow, this remembering stuff was detailed.

She shook herself away from this thought and tried to bring her focus back to the conversation she was having with a groggy Adam, who seemed to be having trouble keeping up with the details she'd been giving him.

"Yes, I'm telling you, someone has been killed in the motel. Or is about to be? It was the lion-head door knockers that tipped me off. I remember seeing a lion painted on the logo. Each knocker on the room doors were brass lion's heads. It's called the Lion's Gate Motel, and it's out by the highway."

She almost rattled off the address and phone number and stopped herself only just in time. Of course, he knew where the motel was and could likely get the number for himself.

"I'd ask how you know all these details, but I understand your visions can be quite…helpful. Little witch, you are sure about these details?"

Little witch. His nickname for her usually made her smile. Today though, Annie was struggling to focus on what he was saying. Was he questioning the details? Details were all she had. Tons of them. Too many. Of course, she was sure.

He must have caught something in her silence because he quickly added, "I'm not doubting you. History has proven to me a few times now to trust your dreams or visions or whatever you call them. I'm … well…concerned. I didn't hear anything last night, but I can check with the desk sergeant. I'll ring you to confirm if something is happening at that motel."

It was all Annie could ask for. Her frustration was more to do with what she still hadn't seen in the visions: anyone other than the victim. She'd gone back into the same images, starting this time at the bar, but her inner camera had kept focused on the woman, on how she'd smiled and flirted. The scene had shifted there to the hallway outside the hotel room. She would never have recognized the place if she hadn't seen the lion's head knockers. The rows of doors and the lack-luster orange carpet looked like a million other such places. She remembered the door knockers when she'd stopped by the hotel before on another case.

She remembered a lot of things right now. She was pretty sure she knew where she'd lost her apartment keys six years ago for the place she'd had in Boston. It was a shame, sort of, that she couldn't go and check.

In the meantime, this seemed like a good time to get caught up on tedious tasks she'd been putting off, which required much thinking. The wheels of justice did not generally grind along at warp speed. With this in mind, she pulled out the files to get caught up on her bookkeeping. No time like the present for paying bills. She even considered whether this might be a good time to shop for a better auto insurance deal.

Two hours later, she was ready to go out. Even with a detail-oriented mind, sitting and staring at numbers all day was impossible. So far, Adam hadn't called back, and her boss at the security firm had been pretty adamant that he needed her to come in today though she'd tried to get out of it. Getting the morning off had been the best she could do. Looking back, she wondered if she'd given too detailed an explanation.

"I have a few more notes to put together for the Gilbert's case file, but I'll finish that work when I get back from running a couple of errands for the community center." She'd only kept herself from explaining just what those errands might be. While her boss, Murphey, might have appreciated the additional explanation, she might have triggered his curiosity more than she had already. She usually didn't give long reasons for needing time off.

This potion is going to be the end of me yet.

Thankfully, Adam called then, giving her a new distraction.

"I might have something. Can you be ready to go in ten minutes?"

"I'll be waiting by the door."

She hung up, smiling. She had been able to hear in his voice the eagerness to track down the root of what she'd been seeing. While he might complain about her visions sometimes, it was all in a teasing way. She knew he lived for these escapades, where they could work together and do some serious good for the town.

Minutes later, she was in his car on the way to the hotel.

His eyes were bright when he picked her up, giving no hint that he hadn't had more than two hours of sleep. "You were right. Something happened at Lion's Gate Motel. Don't know exactly what yet, but we'll find out when we get there, I suppose."

"Murder?"

He shook his head. "They haven't found a body. A lot of blood in the room, though. The sheets were soaked with it. But no corpse of fractions thereof. But that's only in the room. The guys are searching the grounds."

They arrived within minutes, one of the advantages of living in a small town. You were never more than a few minutes from anywhere. Police cruisers were blocking the main entrance to the motel parking lot. Adam drove on the grass to get around them. Annie was out of the car almost before it had come to a complete stop. She didn't know how long the memory-enhancing potion would last before it wore off, and she wanted to get every detail.

With her credentials and Adam backing her up, Annie could get a peek into the hotel room. He was right. There was a great deal of blood everywhere. She remembered the woman screaming in her dream, the 9-1-1 call. They'd been too late, after all, to save anyone.

But the body. Where could it be?

She didn't have long to wait. A few minutes later, an officer called Adam to come down to an abandoned tract of land next to the hotel. In what looked to be an old garden plot, officers searched the tangle of weeds. Annie followed, listening to their conversation with avid interest.

"Here, sir. We've found something. It would likely have belonged to a woman and seems recent. We'll have it for you in a moment."

One of the investigators finished taking pictures of something in the tall weeds. Annie's mouth went dry as she waited, wondering what they had. They appeared to be focused on something relatively minor.

She had her answer a minute later when they finished with the scene, and someone used a long stick to lift what they'd found free of the overgrowth. A bra dangled from the other end of the branch, bright against the dead weeds around it.

"It looks quite new," Adam remarked, coming over to examine it.

"It looks quite expensive," Annie corrected, taking note of the fine stitching and superior materials. She knew for a fact she didn't own anything near that nice, and she didn't exactly go for the cheap stuff regarding her lingerie budget. At least not since Adam had come into her life.

The officer handled the piece of lingerie gingerly before putting it into an evidence bag. "Think it belongs to the woman who made the 9-1-1 call?"

Adam shot Annie a look that she couldn't help but notice, even if the officer they were talking to didn't. She gave a micro shrug. There was no way she could know. Her visions hadn't taken her that far.

Adam took the bag from the officer and turned it over in his hands thoughtfully as he peered through the plastic at what was inside. "Thanks, Marc. Anything else?"

Marc nodded. "Just footprints over the grass, but nothing the forensic guys could identify."

No, they wouldn't. Annie could easily see that something heavy had come through the dense vegetation, but it hadn't rained in ages meaning there would be no prints of notice. There wasn't much anyone could tell from crushed plants and broken leaves.

They truly had a mystery on their hands.

They were about to go when another officer approached from the motel office. "Sheriff, we're in luck. There's a security camera in the parking lot. They caught a car coming in last night, about midnight. A light-colored sedan, Toyota. The plate says it belongs to a Steven Langdon."

CHAPTER 3

The trip back to the station seemed more sedate and quieter, though that was likely a trick of his imagination. The drive was filled with introspection and discussion, which somehow made it feel slower. Something about going out to a call gives some anticipation, never knowing what will be there waiting. Going back was almost anti-climactic.

"So, what now?" Annie seemed to share his mood.

He turned to Annie for a moment and then focused on the road again. "Now...I try to find out this mystery girl's name, where she's from, and whatever I can find. Then I need to talk to this..." he pried the name from his memory, "Steven Langdon. See why he was there. What he knows."

"From Lexington," Annie mused. "Lexington is a rather posh area. You'd think someone from there could afford a nicer hotel. I mean, he could have taken her someplace better. Anyplace would have been better than that one."

"Nice motels ask questions."

They drove for a moment in silence. "Do you think that this guy is maybe...kinky? I mean, he spends the night with a beautiful woman in a cheap dive and then gets his jollies by killing her and slicing her up?" Annie asked in a small voice. The thought of it seemed to make her slightly ill. Of course, seeing the victim in her visions would have brought it home to her. Made it personal. Adam glanced at her from the corner of his eye and saw she was desperately hoping she was wrong. The problem was that he couldn't be quite reassuring as she needed him to be. Not when he was thinking the same thing.

He shrugged. "Don't know. It's possible, been known to happen. But..." he took a breath and tried to piece together the ideas that were only half-formed in his mind, "I don't think it's that simple. I think there's more to this than just some crazy getting satisfaction off some fetish." He considered the thoughts that had been niggling at him for a moment. "There's nobody, for one thing. That's not typical, as far as I know, in extreme cases like that. I mean, there has to be a reason for the lack of a corpse."

The car turned the light, and Annie sat quietly, apparently trying to take his words into account. "But...what? Why?"

"That is the question I want to answer. The first thing I need to do is find and interview this, Steven Langdon."

The rest of the drive was silent between them. It was a companionable silence; both lost in their private musings. It was also a comfortable silence when no one felt obligated to keep the conversation going when just being with the other person was enough.

"Hey, Sheriff." The desk sergeant called by way of greeting as they came in. "You have a visitor. In your office." He thrust a thumb toward the back of the station. "Guy by the name of..." he checked a notepad on his desk, "Langdon. Steven Langdon."

Sherriff Parker exchanged glances with Annie. She shrugged. Even she hadn't seen this coming. "Ah...put him in the interrogation room. I'll be right there." The desk sergeant nodded and picked up his phone. Parker pulled Annie over to one side. "I want you to observe from outside of the room. There's a monitor in the next room; you can get a camera feed. See if you can get any...feelings." It was the wrong word, but he was still unsure what to call whatever she did.

He led her to the observation room and turned on the monitor in time to see a tall, thinnish-looking man being led into the room. Parker stopped at his desk, grabbed a clipboard and the little information he had on the missing woman, and entered the room.

"Mr. Langdon." He held out his hand, "Sheriff Adam Parker. It's a pleasure to meet you, though I have to admit I am somewhat surprised to find you here."

Langdon shook his hand. It was a firm grip but not painful, as if he had something to prove. "My pleasure, Sherriff. I heard about…well, the goings on at the hotel, and I just figured you'd have questions for me. I thought I should come in and see if I can be of any help to you."

"We appreciate that." Parker gestured for Langdon to have a seat and took the chair next to him. It was less formal and gave a clearer image to the camera in the room. "Perhaps we can start with the name of the woman."

Langdon shrugged. "Carla Mendes." Langdon's face curled like he just smelled something a little off. "I would be shocked if that was her real name, but it was the name she gave me. Carla Mendes."

"Why did you spend the night in Lion's Gate? Surely there were more…accommodating places?"

"I don't really know. She was fairly insistent that we go to her place. I might have insisted, but I honestly couldn't believe my luck in the first place; I didn't want to blow it by putting down her hotel. I think she wanted to be 'home,' as it were, and I was a cheap ride." He waved one hand in negation. "To be honest, I would have gladly taken her anywhere away from the crowds. I did offer to take her to my place, but she didn't want to go there. Then she started talking about going away for the weekend. With me. Take a vacation someplace exotic, she said."

"So, what happened after you got to the hotel?"

Langdon shifted in his seat and cleared his throat. "That's…difficult to say. You see…I fell asleep. Early. It's not the sort of thing I do, but I literally could not keep my eyes open. I don't actually know what happened; that's one of the reasons I'm here. I really…don't know."

He took a breath and let the rest out in a rush. "When I woke up, I was alone. There was a considerable amount of blood on the sheets, but…."

"But?" Parker prompted when Langdon didn't finish the thought.

"Well, I thought it was…you know…women's…troubles. I thought maybe she had become embarrassed or something. I mean, it was a lot of blood, but I didn't think it was that much. So I dressed and headed back to town as quickly as I could. I mean…I understand sometimes accidents happen, but to have just left like that…." He shuddered with the memory. "I didn't really think more about it until I heard on the news…anyway, I thought I should come and talk to you about it."

Langdon was cooperative and friendly. Other than claiming to have slept through anything that happened, he answered every question Parker threw at him, even if it meant confessing to a rater's failed assignation with a beautiful woman.

The fact was Parker didn't have enough on him to hold him, and his gut told him that Langdon wasn't his man. He ended up thanking him for coming in and then let him go. Langdon's contact information was on file; they could always get him back when needed. Parker returned to the observation room as one of the uniforms escorted Langdon out.

"So?" He propped himself on a corner of the table that held the monitor and waited for Annie to assess.

Annie slid back from the chair she was sitting on and contemplated the empty room in the monitor. "Adam…I believe him. I don't think he did anything except fall asleep. Remember, in my vision, I saw her. I mean, she was scared and panicky, but she was very much alive. I never saw him," she jabbed a thumb at the monitor, "or anyone else, for that matter, kill her. I didn't even see him at all, but from what I saw there, I don't think he did it."

"I'm inclined to agree with you." Adam set the clipboard down on the table. "That doesn't leave us much." He crossed his arms and lifted an eyebrow. "What do you make of the bra we found? Or all the blood in the room and no dead body?"

Annie thought for a moment and then met his eyes. "I think we need to visit Carla's place and see what else we can find."

It was a good idea and exactly what he'd been thinking they should do. The Sherriff broke a slow grin. "Do me a favor. Don't run for sheriff; you'd get my job."

"No promises," Annie grinned and stood. "Especially since I'm going to be fired if I don't get to work myself at some point today. I might run just to make the mortgage."

"Then we better get moving so you don't have to. Shall we go?"

Annie grinned and took his arm. The touch of her hand on his arm made him glad she'd woken him up this morning.

CHAPTER 4

There weren't very many apartment buildings in Turtle Bay that would be considered high-class. Those were located right on the water. These gave a hint of luxury with a view, buildings of only a few stories so as not to spoil that view, identical to the landscaping. Annie had always thought the Turtle Bay Complex was pretentious and a little boring.

To her surprise, this was not where they went.

They went past and followed the road around where it curved, leading away from the water into a moderate, middle-class neighborhood. When the car stopped outside a small building with two floors and a picture window in each corner, she reassessed everything she knew about the case.

This building, dating back to the 1960s at least, boasted of only eight apartments, four up, four down. The cream-colored brick façade was in good repair though, and the interior was meticulously clean when they stepped into the front hallway.

It just wasn't the sort of place where you would expect to find anything expensive, much less a bra which cost a couple of hundred dollars, a fact Annie had discovered by looking it up on her phone when they'd been driving.

Priorities. Just because she likes expensive clothes doesn't mean anything. She might have spent money on a few signature pieces rather than have an expansive wardrobe of cheaply made things. Don't be a snob.

Figuring she was still 'noticing' too much since her potion that morning, Annie decided she needed to back off a little, at least on some details. She allowed personal bias to creep in when she needed to keep her head in the game.

She glanced at Adam, studying the mailboxes next to the door. "She's upstairs. 2-C."

Annie nodded and followed him to the staircase, where she stopped as if she'd just walked into a wall. Only nothing was in front of her, Only the stairs and a lot of air.

"What?"

Adam was watching her from a couple of steps up. It should have been easy to follow, but when she tried again, it was as if the air had grown solid and refused to let her pass. Something which set her hair on end, really didn't want her to go another step.

"Monty?" she whispered the name, looking for the only ghostly presence in her life though she knew this was ridiculous. Monty really couldn't leave her house. This was something altogether different. Something darker. Angrier. Something which didn't live on the stairs was coming down from upstairs just to greet her.

"Adam, we need to stop. There's something wrong in the building. Can you call a janitor or something to see if anything looks off?"

Adam was already shaking his head. "We can ask someone to open the door, Annie, but only if there's no answer. And once he does, it's my responsibility to go in and check the place out. Why? What's wrong?"

Annie bit her lip. It was impossible to explain. Saying some dark energy lurked on the stair seemed silly. At the same time, whatever it was had enough power to hold her back.

Maybe it's not a 'what' so much as a 'who.' Her mind rushed to grab hold of the details. Her old enemy Ambrose Hazelton might be back in town. Could he possibly set up this kind of trap? What kind of spell would solidify air and not allow a specific person not to pass?

Unless it wasn't specific or a spell. Just her own body's reluctance to go any further.

It isn't supposed to work this way. None of this is supposed to work this way.

Her silent complaint went unheard. Thankfully, whatever was holding her back also disappeared. She staggered, not expecting the sudden freedom, and had to grab the railing to steady herself.

Adam gave her a look and turned back toward the stairs.

Upstairs, the building was quiet. A faint smell of cooked onions hovered near one door. A cat meowed somewhere, sounding like it wanted to be let outside. 3-C was in the back corner on the left. When they knocked, no one answered.

"Well, that settles it," Adam said, and Annie nodded. They would have to wait for the landlord.

Thankfully, he lived just down the street.

"I own all the buildings on this side of the road. Five apartment buildings like this, tucked between residences. Nice places. I keep nice places."

"It seems that way," Annie murmured politely as the man got out a key to the place and shoved it in the lock. A moment later, they were standing just inside the doorway, taking in the enormous disaster which had left furniture overturned and belongings scattered in all directions.

It's as though a hurricane had passed through. Annie glanced toward the kitchen, seeing open cabinets, the contents rifled. A shattered glass lay on the counter.

"This doesn't look like the usual mess an untidy person might leave. It feels like someone tore through here in a hurry," she said thoughtfully.

Adam had been going from room to room clearing the place though it was apparent the apartment was empty. He jerked his head to the side, indicating she should join them. The landlord stayed behind, staring at the mess in dismay. "Do I call the cops or something?"

"I am the cops," Adam reminded him and, shaking his head, gestured for Annie to come into the room.

If anything, the mess was more pronounced here. The closet door stood open, with only a few scattered outfits still on their hangers. A safe beside the bed was open, shelves notably empty.

"I'd say the lady of the house seems to have flown the coop," Adam said, and Annie nodded.

Still unsure what had been trying to force her to stay out of the room, Annie reached out with her senses, trying to see if her intuition was trying to tell her anything. What was it she was supposed to notice?

Or are we not supposed to notice?

She felt a pull that drew her back into the living room. She drifted around the room carefully, knowing it was a crime scene and that she wasn't supposed to touch anything. At the desk, she paused.

Here.

She tugged open a drawer, then opened the next, finding nothing other than a handful of receipts.

There inside was a small, spiral-bound notebook.

"Adam, I might have found something."

Carefully she picked up the book. The first pages seemed to be nothing more than reminders. To-do lists with items crossed out. A reminder to call the dentist and make an appointment. Unsure what she was looking for she kept flipping through. A name stood out, alone on a page with a phone number.

ALEX VENTRY: PRIVATE INVESTIGATOR

A quick glance over at Adam showed he was talking to the landlord rather intently. Not wanting to wait until he was free, Annie grabbed her phone and dialed the number. A man picked up on the first ring.

"Hi, Alex. My name is Annie Archer. I'm a friend of Carla Mendes. I'm at her apartment right now, but she's not here. Any idea where she might have gone?"

Silence. For a moment, she thought he had hung up. When the man spoke again, his words were terse. "I'll be there in five," he said and hung up.

Adam gave her a sharp look from across the room. "What's that all about?"

"I'm impulsive. What else can I say?" she answered with a shrug as the landlord walked into the kitchen, his phone out to take pictures. "What's he doing?"

"Recording damage. I assume to justify keeping the deposit." Adam crossed the room to join her and flipped through the notebook, stopping on the page with the number of the detective. "This the guy you called?"

Annie grimaced. "Not that he told me anything over the phone. I wonder why Carla needed to employ an investigator?"

A tall thin man with dark hair appeared in the open doorway which led to the hallway. "Let me answer that." He came in, hand outstretched for Annie, then Adam to shake. "Alex Ventry."

Adam introduced them both, explaining who he was and that Annie was with him as a special consultant in the investigation. "We appreciate anything you can tell us."

Alex cut right to the chase. "Ms. Mendes has hired me to find the money Mr. Harrison embezzled from Ascot and Associates, an investment firm in town." Alex looked around him, his gaze lingering on the scattered debris. "But as I can see, both subjects have escaped, haven't they?"

CHAPTER 5

Sheriff Harper took a moment to let the information sink in. "And what connection did she have to this Harrison?"

Alex lifted an eyebrow. "The most primitive kind. This is where they would meet at least once each week. During my investigations, I discovered that he was paying for the apartment. She had no expenses at all, really. He was what you'd call a sugar daddy."

Annie frowned. "Wait. You're telling me that Carla was having an affair with this Harrison?" It seemed apparent, but in an investigation, the "obvious" had to be stated in so many words. Assumptions could prove costly, especially if the information were later needed in a trial.

Alex nodded and threaded his thumbs through his belt loops. "Yep. But Harrison was married, so they met exclusively here, in her place." He hesitated for a moment and seemed to reach a decision. "She hadn't paid me, so she's really not my client. She can't claim confidentiality from me anymore. Between us, Sheriff, I'm convinced that Harrison's embezzlement was her idea. She might have even orchestrated the entire thing. I expect she wanted me to establish some kind of trail, a misdirection of the sort."

"Any reason for you to say that?"

"Well, nothing I can produce as evidence, but…the fact she never paid me pretty much guaranteed I'd talk now, didn't it?"

Annie wandered back into the bedroom, leaving the sheriff and the detective alone in the sitting room. Something was playing on her mind: that purse in the vision. She still didn't understand the significance of it, but it kept bothering her.

Nothing made much sense. If Carla was on the run, why bother with a 9-1-1 call? Someone running away does not want to call attention to oneself. For that matter, why involve Langdon in the process if she was on the run with this Harrison fellow? What was the point of the blood unless this Carla was trying to make everyone think she was dead? That made a strange sense; instead of following her, the police would be searching for a dead body.

She stopped short. The purse. It wasn't a purse at all. It was a small suitcase. Carla was already packed up when she made the call. It was a relief to get that memory out, but it was probably not that helpful now; the fact that Carla was on the run was well-known.

She looked around the room for some inspiration, something to trigger…something. A flash caught her eye, something partly under the dresser. She knelt on the floor and teased out a photo from under the furniture.

A Porsche. Beautiful. It flashed in her mind, nearly painful. The vision was so strong. She snatched it up and ran back to where the others were talking. She thrust the picture into the hands of the private eye. "Is this Harrison's car?"

The PI took the photo and studied it. "Yes. That's it." He looked at her as if she had lost her mind. "Why?"

"Because."

Annie refused to take the picture back. It felt…wrong. "Because if you find the car, you find Harrison." Sheriff Harper took the picture and looked closely at the image. "He's dead," Annie said flatly. She knew it as certainly as she knew her own name. That was the flash she had felt, Harrison's death.

"Excuse me," Harper said to the PI, "I should have introduced you more properly. This is Annie Archer. When I introduced her as a consultant, I might have neglected to say in what capacity. She offers…

insights and is a former consultant using these skills to benefit the Turtle Bay Police department."

"Really?" Alex gave her a reassessing look. "You're like one of those psychics?"

"No, I'm...I...."

Adam nudged her. Annie bristled a bit. That was something she had been fighting for years, that horrid label "psychic." She had some abilities, but that put her on the level with 1-900-Dial-a-Vision, and she wasn't comfortable at all with that association. On the other hand, Adam clearly had a reason for letting this man think that of her, so she bit her tongue and let it go...for now.

"Suffice it to say that if Ms. Archer says he'd dead, you can believe he's dead." He looked at the photo again. "Let's see if we can find the car."

"It's in space number 2." Annie pointed to the small parking structure next to the building. Alex looked to the Sheriff for confirmation, who only shrugged and tipped his head in that direction.

The Porsche was easy enough to spot; the black and red sleekness of the car stood out in a garage full of mid-level vehicles.

"That's his." Alex nodded. "Gorgeous car, isn't it?"

"Yeah, it is, but right now, it's evidence. I'll have to have it impounded."

"Not yet." Annie held her hand flat over the car as she walked its length. "It's not just evidence, Adam...." She reached down to the latch in front of the vehicle; the trunk was partly open. "It's a very expensive coffin." She threw the lid to the trunk upward.

"I presume this is Mr. Harrison?" She turned to Alex, who was looking a bit green.

"Yeah. That's him. Was."

Harrison had been there for hours, at least. It was all Annie could take, and she retreated to the back of the car to get some air that wasn't tainted by the smell of death.

Was that what she felt on the stairs? Was that somehow connected to the late Mr. Harrison? That didn't make sense either, not really. He would want to be found, wouldn't he? Why block them...her from discovering the body and ensuring he had a decent funeral?

Or was it something quite the opposite? Harrison's spirit is so desperate to be discovered that he hadn't wanted her to waste time in the apartment but had instead been trying to pull her to him here so he could be found.

The poor man. Embezzler or not, he certainly hadn't deserved this.

Adam called it in, coroner, impound tow, crime scene investigation. In a few minutes, the entire garage would be locked down tightly. So would the apartment. Not that it mattered, they had exhausted every clue they could get from this place. Harrison wasn't going to be testifying, but everything needed to be logged, checked, and carefully documented.

Meanwhile, Carla was out there. Somewhere. Everything they were gathering, all the evidence in the world, wasn't going to do much unless she was caught.

Annie tried to clear her mind.

It occurred to her that she was the only one who knew with certainty that Carla was still alive. Meaning Carla had to be pretty confident about now.

It also meant they still had a chance to catch her.

CHAPTER 6

Things moved pretty quickly from there. The forensic guys showed up to process the apartment. Annie finally made it to work, knowing full well that it would take hours for them to examine the evidence, remove the body, and finally tow the car to the impound lot as evidence. Not that she was overly productive once she got to work. Her mind was on the case as she wondered just what the evidence would show.

The following day, they had at least some answers. Mr. Harrison had been dead for twelve to fifteen hours, coinciding with the time Carla had placed her 9-1-1 call. Annie showed up at police headquarters shortly after she got the news, eager to go over the evidence with Adam and hopefully to add a little of her insight to the matter.

"So, it looks like she must have died at the same time. A partner, perhaps? Someone who took out Harrison to get the money and went after Carla as soon as they realized what she knew?"

"No," Annie said firmly. "Carla is alive and well." She picked up a photograph of the woman from the scattered pages of the police file, which lay across the desk in front of her. "I know it."

"You can tell that from her photo?" Adam asked. "I didn't know your powers could do that."

"I know it from the evidence. Think about it. She'd led you to believe she's dead from the breadcrumbs she's left for you to follow. The bra. The blood."

"It was her blood though…they typed and matched with data from her medical records."

"Menstrual cups. Don't make that face, Adam; it's a perfectly natural thing. I would suspect, though, that she collected her own blood to cover her tracks. It's easy enough to do, and there wasn't near enough blood there to account for a murder. Even the M.E. agreed on that."

Adam thought about this for a minute. "So, we were looking for a body between the blood and the bra. What you saw was her phony 9-1-1 call. She was never being attacked at all."

"No. I suspect she returned to town knowing full well the detective she'd hired was off duty for the night." She rifled through the papers and found Alex's official police statement. "According to his statement, he'd gone to sleep when he knew Harrison was home at his apartment and had gone to bed. She must have lured him to the garage on some pretense and killed him there."

"Sounds about right. What happened after that?" A middle-aged woman with dark hair and olive skin stood in the doorway. "Agent Morgan. FBI. I believe you were expecting me." She offered her ID.

Adam rose to greet her and offered her a chair at the conference table where they'd spread out everything from the police file. Annie smiled at the older woman, liking her instantly. "The rest should be fairly easy to guess. I imagine she went upstairs, changed her clothes, packed, and took off with her suitcase in tow. I expect she was rattled, never having killed a man before, hence the mess in the apartment. She was panicking probably and wanted to get as far from there, as quickly as possible."

Adam nodded. "The crime lab is going over her computer now, trying to figure out her travel plans."

"We might not need them," Annie said, picking through the photographs again and coming to rest on one taken from her desk. "That there…" she pointed to an empty cartridge box for the printer laying on the floor next to the chair. "Were there any papers taken from the apartment? Trash, maybe?"

"I get what you're looking for," Agent Morgan said with a smile and nodded toward a box that hadn't been opened yet. "In there, maybe?"

Adam pulled the lid off the box. The notebook they'd gotten Alex's information from was on top. Underneath were some crumpled papers. "This what you're looking for?" He pulled out a poorly printed sheet, with streaks throughout the document indicating the ink had run out halfway through the job. What remained was barely legible.

"Is that a rental agreement of some kind?" Agent Morgan asked with interest.

"Charter for a boat," Annie said with sudden insight. "Destination Paris."

"A private charter yacht?" Adam asked, immediately grabbing for his phone. "I'll get someone on it. Maybe the coast guard can catch up before they hit international waters."

"Or we can extradite from whatever ports the boat shows up on the way." Agent Morgan had her phone out as well. "We'll have to get some other government agencies in on this."

Hours later, the yacht was finally spotted off the coast of Aruba. "She can catch a direct flight from there to France," Annie said when they told her.

"Already on it. We're working with the local authorities both there and in France. They'll catch her, and she'll be arrested if she's got the money with her."

It didn't sound right. Annie paced around her house after she hung up, wondering what they were missing. Monty watched her in concern and mimicked sleeping as if telling her to try going to bed to see if she could get further insight from her dreams.

Only Annie didn't need to sleep to see things. She'd had visions before while waking, and she still had some of the potion left, which would give her that fine attention to detail. The aftereffects had annoyed her for hours after the last time she'd tried it, but wasn't it worth it in the end?

She called Adam and asked him to come over.

"Normally, I wouldn't try this with someone else in the room," she explained when she got there, "but I'm afraid I might see something which is time-sensitive, and I need you to be able to act quickly if that happens."

"You're sure it's safe?" Adam asked, touching her hand lightly with his own, his eyes full of affection and no small amount of concern.

"It's safe," she assured him with a kiss and settled herself quietly in the chair she's used before. With a reassuring smile for Adam, she took the potion and opened herself to the vision again the way she had last time. She wondered if she would just see the same scenes again, the hotel room or even the bar. Instead, she saw the yacht floating in the darkness just offshore from what looked like a busy port. A woman stood at the rail watching the approaching lights from police cruisers. Frantic, she raced to the opposite rail, her eyes on another yacht anchored not far away. It was clear to see she was going to jump.

Annie jolted herself out of the vision. "Adam, she's still on board the boat. I think she's going to jump overboard. I can see her swimming…I think she's too far from the beach. There was another boat." She gave as many details as she could remember. Thankfully with the help of the potion, this was quite a lot. She even captured part of the boat's name and several letters painted on the stern.

"I'm on it."

She waited with him while he made the call. When he was done, he sat beside her, sliding an arm around her shoulders. Annie was shaking.

"It'll be okay."

"I'm not so sure. The money…what if it's lost?"

"Did you see it in the vision?"

She shook her head. Carla's hands had been empty. "By now, it's probably in an offshore account." Her tone was mournful. Had they come so far only to end up with nothing at all?

Two days later, Carla Mendes, alias Angela Regent was brought back to America to face charges of murder, fraud, embezzlement, and many others. It seemed this wasn't her first time using a man to embezzle funds from a company. It was the first time she'd been forced to kill to get away.

While it was gratifying to see the end of the case and know she'd done something important in helping to solve it, Annie couldn't help but feel like she could have done something more. She'd been warned about what Carla would do several times that night. It had simply taken her too long to figure out what she was seeing. Could she have prevented a death if she'd only acted sooner? Or had she been shown what was set in stone, what was fated to happen?

The philosophical and even moral issues of all this troubled her. She wanted to know why she was shown these visions at all. Everything had been changing so rapidly in the past year. Why was this happening to her?

She tucked these worries away and told herself she needed to move on. After all, she and Adam had done considerable good with what she'd seen. With the capture of Carla, or Angela, they had locked away a dangerous woman.

As for her visions…well, maybe she'd be given a chance to do better in her next adventure.

The End

MIDSUMMER MISCHIEF

A MYSTIC MOONHAVEN MYSTERY

CHAPTER 1
SOLSTICE SHADOWS

Ella, my best friend, eyed my drumming fingers as she stopped by the table I occupied all by myself in her coffee shop. "Harper, I think you've had enough coffee. Why not switch to decaf?"

I forced my hand to lie flat, then heaved a sigh. "Coffee has nothing to do with it."

Ella's eyes widened as she glanced around. Ella's Wheel was packed today. She leaned in close and lowered her voice. "Is it magic or Liam?" she asked.

Normally, I would find her questions endearing. They reminded me that someone in this town cares about me despite being a relatively recent addition. I'd only lived in Moonhaven for about eighteen months now. While I had a solid group of friends, I was still the whacky newcomer with the weird occult bookstore. Thankfully, I'd recently moved into the small studio over the store I'd been working on for the past three months. The less people knew about my private life, the better.

"It's not Liam," I grumbled. The lie was obvious even to me.

Detective Liam Ashford was one of those friends I had in Moonhaven. At least he was. I wasn't sure where we stood in our relationship anymore. Not since he revealed he had been keeping meticulous notes on me with the mysterious happenings in town. It was like a slap in the face… or a threat.

I shook those thoughts off. "Something is off about the magical energy here in town," I whispered so nobody else could hear me. "It's just like the other times. I think something is going to happen."

Ella's brows pinched together in worry. "You need to talk to Liam about it."

"I can't."

Ella sucked on her teeth and then pointed toward the door that led into the back. "Go upstairs. I'll be up in a minute to talk."

I almost protested—I had to get back to my bookstore. But business had been lackluster for the last month. People were more interested in getting outdoors and in the sun than they were in reading. So I shrugged and headed into the back, where I waved at the baker and trudged upstairs. Her upstairs apartment was decorated in shades of blue and green, creating a soothing underwater vista.

Ella joined me shortly. She put her honey-brown hair up into a bun and plopped onto the couch next to me. I grabbed a seashell-shaped pillow and hugged it to my chest, lowering my chin as I stared at the floor.

"What's going on? You two have been on the outs for weeks," Ella said. "And I don't get it."

My nose wrinkled. "After what happened during the May Day festival, Liam showed me a notebook he'd been keeping. He's been studying me, taking notes, connecting me to everything that's been happening. It's like he thinks I'm responsible."

"Did you tell him the truth?"

I shook my head. "I can't tell him about magic. I shouldn't even have told you and Max. The only reason I did was because I had no other choice."

Ella's brow furrowed. "Max is a witch, too, though."

"Doesn't matter. He'll tell you the same thing. We're not supposed to tell anyone."

"Alright." She looked unconvinced but, to her credit, didn't push. "What can I do to help, then?"

"Keep an eye out and let me know if you or anyone else notices anything strange that happens around town."

"I can do that. I am, after all, manager of the Moonhaven Rumor Mill," she said, then laughed.

Ella loved gossip, and everyone knew she did. She'd never spread things that could actually hurt people, though. It was one reason I loved her so much.

We headed back downstairs, finding the shop a little emptier than it had been when Ella took her break. My table had been taken by Abigail, my former landlady who ran the B&B across the street... and Liam. I hesitated. I wanted to talk to Abigail, but I could do that later, right?

On the other hand, I shouldn't let Liam drive me away from the things I liked.

I headed over. "Hi, Abigail."

"Harper." She smiled at me. "I saw your store was closed for lunch and thought you might be here."

Liam looked distinctively unhappy to see me. He stared down at the coffee in his hands, his usually calm and relaxed demeanor tense.

"Well, I'm headed back to the store now," I told Abigail. "If you want to stop by to chat, I'd love to."

I headed for the door. A chair scraped against the floor behind me and a prickly sensation washed over the back of my neck, but I didn't stop. Liam caught up with me on the sidewalk.

"Harper, wait," he called.

I slowed down and glanced back at him. "What?"

"I just want to ask how you're doing," he said.

I turned back to him, folding my arms. He was a handsome man and the puppy-dog eyes he was giving me right now made me falter. I took a deep breath and reminded myself of what he did. "You watch me so closely. You should already know how I'm doing."

I tightened my arms around myself. I was supposed to be his friend, not a suspect. Why should I be the first to apologize when he hadn't apologized to me?

Liam opened his mouth, and I found I didn't even want to hear an apology. That really was unfair of me, I know, but I was still angry. I turned on my heel and walked away without waiting to hear what he had to say.

I almost hoped he'd follow. But he didn't.

I got back to my store and flung open the door, stomping inside, only to stop dead when I saw it wasn't empty. A woman sat in the middle of the floor, rocking back and forth in a rocking chair that hadn't been there a moment ago. Her hair was the same shade of gray as Abigail's, with big brown eyes. She wore clothes that reminded me of the early sixteen hundreds.

I swallowed hard as I met the woman's eyes. She had a slightly transparent quality to her and the rocking chair made no noise against the hardwood floor.

"What are you doing here?" I asked as I closed the door behind me.

"I never found out what happened to my daughter, and the veil has been mighty thin between Moonhaven and the other side this year," the woman replied. She sounded as though she could have stepped in from outside, rather than coming from another century. "The name's Gail Blackwood."

My eyes widened. "Penelope's mother?"

She nodded once.

I studied her. Her large eyes were hard and wary, as though she had had a very hard life. There was something familiar about them, though. I automatically thought of David Blackwood, the museum curator. But before I could study his face in my memory, another one arrived in my mind. Abigail Thorne.

"Is your full name Abigail, by any chance?" I asked.

"Yes. I go by Gail, though." Gail rocked harder. "If you can help me find my daughter, let me know. Otherwise, stay out of my way."

She disappeared with a chill wind.

I shivered, despite the heat of midsummer. Outside, everything was in bloom, but the interior of my shop was cold now, even though my AC didn't work that great. I hesitated a moment before I closed my eyes and opened my palms. I sent out my searching winds, and they came back with the distinctive feeling of a spirit's lingering presence.

I'd had some false positives in the past, but this time I was certain.

Gail Blackwood's spirit had come to Moonhaven. Was it just a coincidence that she shared the same name as the B&B owner?

This gave me something to focus on, though. The uneasy energy I'd been feeling around town lately could very well be related to Gail.

I headed back to Ella's Wheel. Abigail was still there talking with Liam, and I hesitated. It could wait. I didn't have anything that needed to be resolved right at this exact second. I didn't need to face off with Liam again.

On the other hand, why should I let him control what I did? If he wanted to take notes on my actions, he could. It wasn't as though he was going to figure out I was talking to ghosts just because I asked Abigail a few questions.

I stepped inside and headed over to their table. "Abigail, I forgot I wanted to ask you something. I've been looking into the Penelope Blackwood thing again lately, and I learned that her mother's name was Gail. Do you have any family history in Moonhaven?"

"If there is, I'm not aware of it," Abigail said, raising her eyebrows toward her hairline. She frowned at me, as though she wasn't happy that I'd even asked. "My father moved us to Moonhaven when I was young."

There was a slightly sharp note to her voice. Was she being cagey or was she chastising me for interrupting her conversation with Liam?

"Why do you ask?" Liam asked me.

I wrinkled my nose. "I'm just curious. Abigail, I'm going to close up shop for the rest of the day. I'm going to the museum to catch up with David, and I'll stop by the B&B later to chat. Okay?"

"Yes, that's fine," Abigail said.

Liam shot me a frustrated look. I ignored it as I turned away once more. He had my number. He could text me an apology at the very least. It didn't have to be this big scene, nor did he have to be alone with me to apologize. Maybe he was frustrated, but he only had himself to blame for taking notes on me as though I was a criminal.

If I was completely honest with myself, though, I'd admit that it wasn't just an apology that I was looking for. When he gave me that notebook and I asked him why he did that, he hadn't answered. Only told me I needed to tell him everything.

As though I could! I wanted to tell him. I wanted to share all the strange things, the connections between them, and the way I kept digging up more and more about Moonhaven's past. It killed me to have to keep everything hidden away like this.

But I had to. I couldn't tell him.

Tell no one. That was a witch's creed. And I'd broken it out of necessity with Ella, when a spell was killing her. Liam didn't need to know. He couldn't know. I could never tell him anything.

And so how was this gulf between us ever supposed to close?

CHAPTER 2
ENCHANTED EVENING

Moonhaven didn't have any official celebrations for the midsummer solstice, but that didn't mean that there weren't private celebrations.

Anabel Marley, our new mayor whom Liam and I had rescued from the old mayor during the events of May Day —long story— welcomed me into her home that evening. She was dressed in a gown with layers of different shades of green, with a delicate tiara made to look like flowers and branches perched on her head. She beamed at me as she hugged me.

"I'm so glad you made it, Harper," Anabel gushed. "Come on in. The party's getting started. We have board games in the dining room, dancing in the living room, and, of course, plenty of coffee, energy drinks, and other things to keep us awake through the shortest night of the year!"

"Always glad to party," I replied with a laugh.

Everyone was dressed in the 'fantasy woodland' theme that Anabel had decorated her house with. There were a few people, who, like Anabel, dressed like a forest nymph. Most people stuck various types of ears on their heads. Some people were more like Peter Pan or Robin Hood.

I'd worn a green shirt and brown pants. Not very woodland now that I saw the lengths other people went to, but at least I matched the general décor.

I wandered into the living room, where there was less dancing and more standing around the edges of the room, listening to music and chatting. As I looked around, I saw David Blackwood. We'd talked earlier at the museum and I was about to see if Ella had arrived yet when I realized who David was talking to… Liam.

They seemed engrossed in their conversation as I made a beeline for them. What could they be talking about? Liam didn't seem to be interested in Moonhaven's history. Was he checking up on me because I said I was going to visit the museum earlier?

"What are you two talking about?" I asked when I arrived next to them.

David jumped, as though he hadn't realized I was there. Liam sipped at whatever he was drinking, his blue eyes not leaving David's face. He gave no indication I was even there.

"Liam was just seeing if I'd found more information on Penelope Blackwood for you," David explained. "I was telling him that so far there's nothing to indicate she ever returned to Moonhaven."

My shoulders tensed. What was Liam checking up on me like this for? I had hoped, in the few seconds it took me to get over here, that I was just being paranoid. Yet it seemed like it was, in fact, a valid concern.

I struggled to keep my expression smooth. "I hardly expected you to find anything after just a few hours."

David laughed. "True, but I've found a few promising leads. I've actually been looking more into the Blackwood family tree since January. I've found quite a bit of interesting things concerning her genealogy. I'll have a package for you tomorrow about everything."

"Thanks." I wasn't sure how genealogy would help me find out what exactly happened to Penelope Blackwood, but it was something.

Four hundred years ago, Howard Whitman had used magic to make Penelope disappear, then claimed that they had been married so he could inherit all the lands that belonged to her. I thought it was pretty likely that she had been killed, but maybe there was a way to find her bones and bring Gail some peace… and if Gail, being on the other side, didn't know what happened to her daughter then maybe Penelope was still lingering around here on the mortal plane somewhere.

In any case, I could help. So long as Liam didn't mess things up.

"Do you mind if I talk with Detective Ashford for a moment alone?" I asked David.

He moved off, and I pulled Liam closer to the corner before I turned on him. "What do you think you're doing?"

"You're acting strange again." His usually expressive eyes were blank.

I folded my arms. "Strange?"

"The last few days you've been twitchy and short-tempered," he said, mirroring me. "You've been looking into the history of the town again, and you only do that when something weird is about to happen. You're acting the same way you did before everything else that happened."

I inhaled sharply through my nose. Even when I wasn't talking to him, he could see what was happening to me. I wanted to say that I hated it, but I had to admit that I was more than a little… I don't know, maybe flattered? I wasn't sure how I was supposed to react to my own feelings.

"I'm not acting strange at all. I'm just mad at you," I told him.

He dropped his arms and reached out, taking my hand lightly. His fingers wrapped around mine as the mask dropped from his face.

Regret was written so deeply in his eyes that it took my breath away.

"I know I scared you with that notebook," he murmured. "And I'm sorry. I didn't mean to. I just want to know the truth about what's happening in Moonhaven. Can't you tell me that?"

The earnestness in his gaze left me wavering. As upset as I still was with him about this whole thing, I missed having him around. I'd gotten used to our morning walks, watching TV together, just hanging out. I hated we had so much of a gulf between us. I didn't want things to get worse.

But he just said exactly why I couldn't fix things. He wanted the truth, which was the one thing that I couldn't offer him.

I turned my face away to hide my emotions, only to stiffen and gasp. There, in the middle of the dancefloor, was Gail Blackwood. Her gaze was laser-focused on a young woman I vaguely recognized. Her name was Chloe, I thought—she came into my store every so often looking for new romances. She was dancing with a young man.

Before I could go over, though, the music cut out. Anabel stood next to the speakers, and she clapped her hands. "Twilight is officially over. It's now the night! Let's all step outside for some fireworks."

Gail disappeared. I started forward, hoping to get to Chloe as everyone streamed from the house. But even as I did so, Liam tugged on my hand. He hadn't let go, and I hadn't pulled away. I bit my lip as I turned back toward him.

"What's happening?" he demanded.

I stared into his dark blue eyes, and the truth lingered on the tip of my tongue. It would be so easy to tell him everything... but then I thought about how he'd look at me if I did tell him everything. He might realize that strange things were happening in Moonhaven, but he had no idea it was on the mystical side of things.

If there was one thing Liam Ashford didn't believe in, it was magic. A bitter laugh caught in my throat. Even if I dared to tell him...

"I can't tell you, and if I did, you wouldn't believe me."

He dropped my hand. "Can't or won't? It makes a difference."

"It does," I agreed. "Which is why when I say I can't tell you, I mean it."

Liam growled softly as he dragged his hand through his hair. The sound startled me; I hadn't realized he was this frustrated! But then, I had been evading him for some time. It was likely that he was just as frustrated as I was by this entire business.

The booming of the fireworks started outside. We both paused, glancing at the window. A burst of light lit the backyard, but none of the fireworks could be seen from this angle. I thought about trying to get back outside, but right now I didn't even want to look at the light show.

"Why?" Liam demanded. "Why can't you tell me?"

"Because of reasons that I can't tell you."

He groaned as he rubbed his hands over his face. "So then I guess I'll just have to keep looking on my own, huh? I'll have to figure out what you're hiding from me."

I closed my eyes, fighting back the urge to snap at him. This wasn't a threat. He was merely stating a fact. Knowing Liam, it was torture for him to have so much that he didn't understand. Could I really blame him for that?

"If you trust me, then you won't," I told him.

"How can I trust you when you're keeping secrets from me?"

"You keep secrets from me, too. You don't tell me everything about the cases you work on."

"That's not the same!" Liam threw his hands into the air. "Those are details I can't tell you. You know that."

I nodded, my heart beating shallowly. This reminded me too much of the fight we'd had when he first showed me his notebook. I hated it. I didn't want to fight with Liam. I wanted this to blow over as though it had never happened in the first place.

"You can't tell me," I agreed. "Which is why it's exactly the same."

Liam searched my face, understanding dawning on his face. Confusion followed quickly. Would it be enough for him to stop asking questions when I couldn't give him answers? Or would it just make him ask even more questions?

"We should go outside," I murmured, my shoulders slumping. "It sounds like the fireworks are already over."

Anabel appeared in the doorway. "There you two are! Have you seen Chloe?"

"Not since everyone went outside," I answered. The worry on Anabel's face sent a chill down my spine. "What happened?"

"I'm sure she's around somewhere. Her boyfriend noticed she was missing and we haven't been able to find her. Her car is still here, though... I don't know where she would have gone to. Maybe she took a walk or something. Or maybe someone drove her home..."

"We'll come look," Liam said, striding forward.

We headed outside. People were calling for Chloe and more than one person grumbled about the party being ruined. I headed to look through the parked cars, thinking maybe she'd taken a breather. There were no answers to my calls, though.

When I got to her car, I caught sight of a fluttering white thing tucked into the handle of the car. I plucked it out, finding a carefully embroidered handkerchief.

My heart sank. The corner had an elaborate 'GB' on it. Gail Blackwood.

Oh, no. Had Chloe been kidnapped by a ghost?

CHAPTER 3
NIGHT OF REVELATIONS

"What do you have there?"

I jumped, whirling. Liam stood a little way down from me, craning his neck toward the handkerchief as he approached. I held it out to him silently. When he took it, his brow furrowed. He turned it over in his hands and looked back up at me.

"I found it in her door handle," I explained.

Liam's expression tightened. "Nobody saw her leave, and I have a funny feeling about all of this. Will you help me find her?"

I twisted my hands together, searching his face in the darkness. The last vestiges of twilight had disappeared, and the night was only broken by a crescent moon hanging above us in the sky. My heart twinged; he was offering an olive branch here, and I wasn't sure if I could take it.

Did this mean he'd accepted that I had things he couldn't know? Or was it—

Gail Blackwood appeared at my elbow, making me jump. She looked around, her expression morphing from confusion to irritation. She turned to me and glanced me up and down. "I wondered what I was hearing. It's you again. I've seen a bunch of your conversations with this man. If you can't trust him, why are you spending so much time with him?"

The air left my lungs, her words as powerful as a punch to the stomach. The warnings my parents drilled into me flooded my mind, but that still rang in my ears.

Did I trust Liam? I'd spent the last six or more months wanting to tell him the truth. But my parents found each other and told one another that they were witches. How could I go through my life constantly hiding that vital part of me?

"What is it?" Liam asked, looking right through Gail.

I opened my mouth to tell him nothing. To continue the lie... but when he looked back at me and our eyes met, I couldn't. I didn't want to keep these secrets from him. I didn't want to keep lying and being frustrated and angry. I didn't want to be the one that made it so this gulf between us couldn't be bridged.

He shared those notes with me for a reason. He wasn't accusing me of anything. It was a plea, an offering.

"You're not going to like it," I said slowly. "And you probably won't believe me."

His brow furrowed.

I sighed as I leaned against the side of Chloe's car. "Ever since I was a child, the one rule that's been drilled into me over and over is never to tell anyone. Let no one know. It's..."

"I thought you said you couldn't tell me," Liam said. His voice was flat.

"I shouldn't, the same way you shouldn't tell anyone about your cases, but technically it's possible." I took a deep breath, preparing to say the words out loud. Why did they feel so heavy on my tongue? "I'm a witch. Everything that's been happening in Moonhaven is magic.

"First it started with the Winter Festival. Percival Whitman used magic to attack David Blackwood. The unnatural frost, the wolves people were seeing? It was all magic. All him. On Valentine's Day, I used magic to figure out the secret messages in those letters."

I paused to get a read on him, but in the darkness, I couldn't see his face clearly. Was any of this having an impact? I plunged on. "On the

Spring Equinox, a collection of curses were weighing down on Ella, because she's a descendant of all the original founders of Moonhaven. Four hundred years' worth of generational curses were going to kill her. The disappearances of artifacts from the museum were related to magic."

"And is magic the reason for my memory loss?" Liam asked. His voice was low and still emotionless. My heart sank somewhere down to my toes. He didn't believe me.

"In a way," I admitted. "You were helping me remove the spell from her when the bell crashed through the ceiling. Magically, that is. It struck your head, and that's what made you forget."

Gail grunted as she folded her arms. "Are you done yet?"

I sighed and gestured to her. "And I'm distracted because Gail Blackwood is standing right here. Her ghost, that is, and I'm suspecting that she has something to do with Chloe's disappearance."

"A ghost?" Liam repeated, the disbelief clear in his voice.

"Why, I never!" Gail glared at me. Unlike Liam, her features were perfectly visible. Her nostrils flared as she shook her finger at me. "I thought you might be useful in looking for my Penelope, but I can see I was mistaken."

"A ghost kidnapped Chloe?" Liam asked again.

I shook my head. "She's saying that she didn't. She wants to find out what happened to Penelope."

Liam shook his head and turned away.

Gail pinched her lips tightly together. "All I want to know is what happened to her. All these years, terrified for her. I haven't even gone to the other side properly, because I just know her spirit is lost. And then you accuse me of doing the same to some other girl's mother?"

"That's not what I meant," I said.

"That's exactly what you said," Gail replied. She continued to glare at me, then vanished.

Liam rubbed his temples. "I don't understand what you're talking about, Harper. How can any of that be true?"

I winced at his words, my stomach swooping. "I told you, you wouldn't believe it."

"Harper—"

"Hey, what are you—" someone came running up next to Liam, only to stop. The flashlight on a cell phone flashed into our faces. I shielded my eyes. "Oh, Detective Ashford. What are you doing here?"

I stepped to one side so the beam of light wasn't blinding me. A young man, the one Chloe had been dancing with, stood a little ways away, along with Anabel, a redheaded woman, and a couple other people I didn't know.

"We were looking for Chloe," Liam replied, his voice smooth. "Any sign of her?"

"Nah, not yet," the man said. He looked over at me. "Aren't you Harper Nightshade?"

I extended my hand. "Sure am. Liam asked me to help him out a bit."

"Trevor. I'm Chloe's boyfriend. And this here is Angelica," he added, gesturing toward the redheaded woman.

"I'm Chloe's best friend," she said, sounding oddly defensive. "She's not in her car, is she? I told her not to go wandering around at night. During the fireworks, she started talking about walking home."

Trevor sighed. "I wouldn't worry too much. She has a habit of running off like this."

Anabel gestured us all back to the house. "Let's get back to the party, shall we? Trevor and Angelica are right. I've known Chloe for a few years. She does like to go off and do her own thing."

Liam and I shared a glance. He tucked the handkerchief into his pocket as we headed back toward the house. We both lingered behind the group, but unfortunately, we would not have any time to talk about what I'd just told him. Trevor stayed back with us.

"Detective, if I'm honest, I think Chloe might have skipped town," he murmured to Liam. "She owes our landlord almost a full year's rent. She's been talking for months about just running off and disappearing. I don't know, but it might be good to have people on the lookout for her in other cities."

"I'll take that into advisement," Liam replied. "But if she was walking back to her home, we'll wait to see if she's even left first."

I frowned at him, but he caught my hand in the darkness as I opened my mouth. He squeezed my fingers, as though telling me to be quiet. I shut my mouth again. I wasn't sure what was going on here, and what any of it had to do with Gail. It must have a connection somewhere, but what was it?

Back at the house, Trevor headed off into the kitchen. Liam leaned close to my ear.

"I'm going to talk with the boyfriend more. You go see what Anabel thinks of Chloe, if this is like her or not," he murmured.

The feeling of his breath against my ear sent shivers down my spine. My heartbeat increased, although there was another reason for that—excitement that maybe Liam did trust me after all. He clearly thought more was happening here than we were being told.

I went off in search of Anabel, finding her in one of the upstairs rooms, where a rather impressive-looking Dungeons and Dragons game was being played.

"Hey, can we talk a bit?" I asked her.

"Sure."

We stepped into the hallway, and Anabel gave me a grin. "What's up?"

"Well…" I shrugged and laughed softly, as though embarrassed. "Honestly, I'm still a little worried about Chloe. Her boyfriend said that she's got some debt issues and may have skipped town."

Anabel leaned against the wall. "Honestly? It wouldn't surprise me. Chloe and I have been friends for a while, but things have been strained between us. I invested in a business venture she proposed, but it fell apart before she could get a start. Chloe is very avoidant of conflict."

"So you think she skipped town?"

"I think she probably got a bit too tipsy and left." Anabel shrugged. "Chloe doesn't like parties. Trevor's the one who insisted she come along. Although…"

"Although what?"

"It's probably nothing," Anabel said, though her expression said otherwise. "It's just that I've noticed a few things between Trevor and Angelica. Small touches, lingering glances. It's probably harmless, but I just get this gut feeling… Oh, but I shouldn't gossip like this."

She shook her head while I turned over what she had just said. If

Chloe's boyfriend and best friend had something going on, maybe she found out about it? That would explain her sudden departure... If that was the case, then maybe she really did just go home, and they were too embarrassed to admit it.

"What about you and the detective?" Anabel asked.

My head jerked up. "What about us?"

She gave me a knowing smile. "I've noticed how the two of you interact, too. So where are you at in your relationship?"

"We're not—" My cheeks turned hot as I spluttered. "There's no relationship."

Her knowing smile increased. "You should be open with him, Harper. He feels the same way. You're only holding yourself back."

I ducked my head. "Er, I have to go."

"I'm sorry if I overstepped," Anabel said.

"I have to go," I repeated.

I hurried back down the stairs, though I couldn't miss the tinkling laugh from Anabel. Honestly! What was that question even about? I smoothed down my shirt as I wove between the partygoers. I spied Liam with Trevor in the kitchen and slipped in, though I ignored them and went to the coffee machine.

"Chloe and I have been having a rough patch," Trevor admitted to Liam. "I was thinking she might step out on me."

"Ahh. And you two decided to be exclusive?" Liam asked.

Trevor shrugged. "We hadn't really talked it through, but yeah, that was where I thought it was."

"So you've been exclusive to her?"

"Whoa." Trevor frowned at him. "I'm not sure any of this is your business."

Liam lifted his hands. "Sorry. I've been drinking a bit and I guess my filter's gone. You're right, it's none of my business. But since she texted you, I suppose there's nothing to be worried about. Harper! I didn't see you."

I jumped and turned with a fresh cup of coffee. Liam grinned at me as he brushed past Trevor to grab my hand. "Ella called. She wants us to stop by. You ready to go?"

I set the coffee down and let him pull me away. As we passed through the doorway, I glanced back at Trevor, who watched us with narrowed eyes. And right beside him was Gail Blackwood.

CHAPTER 4
SECRETS UNDER THE STARS

At Ella's Wheel, I told Liam what Anabel had told me. The coffee shop was empty except for Ella, who we quickly brought up to speed with what was happening. Liam explained that Trevor and Angelica both seemed somewhat rattled, and he wasn't sure that he believed their excuses.

"Don't you have to wait twenty-four hours before you investigate?" Ella asked, resting her elbows on the table.

Liam shook his head. "That's movie nonsense. The first twenty-four hours are crucial to finding the missing person. Although I suppose if magic is involved, there isn't much we can do about it."

I stiffened at his sarcastic tone, but Ella's jaw dropped.

"I thought you couldn't tell him," she said, whirling on me. "Didn't you say that you're not supposed to tell anyone?"

Liam tensed. He narrowed his eyes, not at Ella but at me. "So, you're not supposed to tell anyone, but you told Ella?"

"She was under a spell. I told you that," I said, my hands clenched. "And just because you don't believe me doesn't mean it's not true."

"I never said I don't believe you."

Ella glanced between us, her eyes wide and expression regretful.

A muttered swear behind me made me jump. I turned, heart

hammering, but sagged in relief when I saw it was only Gail. We hadn't just accidentally revealed my magic to yet another person here in Moonhaven. I rubbed my temples.

"Gail Blackwood is back," I said.

"Back?" Ella repeated.

Gail passed through her and sank into the booth. "Why, when I'm trying to look for my daughter, do I keep getting pulled back to you?"

"Hold on a minute," I told her, then turned to Liam and Ella. "This is going to get confusing, listening to one half of the conversation." I leaned over the table toward Gail. "You told me earlier that you haven't gone to the other side. Why not?"

"Because I have to find my daughter."

"But can't you come back over every so often?" I pressed. "The veil is thin around Moonhaven. Can't you peek through?"

Gail shook her head. "It doesn't work like that. At least not for me. I'm stuck in a halfway point, not really here and not really there. Not until I can find my Penelope. I have spent the last four hundred years performing the searching ritual every midsummer."

I rubbed the back of my neck. "Even if you are right and she survived Howard Whitman's attack, it has been four hundred years. Penelope will have died by this time, by old age, if nothing else."

"Yes, she will have. And yet, I haven't even been able to find her bones." Gail groaned as she passed her hand over her eyes. "I can't move on until I know what happened to her. It's the only way I'll find her spirit to bring it home."

I nodded slowly. "So, you've been brought back to Moonhaven every midsummer?"

"My magic is tied closely to the sun and its seasons. But this is the first time anyone in town has seen me or interacted with me," Gail said.

Ella touched my hand. "Catch us up?"

I nodded and explained everything. Liam's expression was hard and blank, like he wasn't sure if he believed any of it. It was about what I expected from him, so I tried my best to ignore the knot growing in the pit of my stomach.

"If Gail has a searching spell, we can use it to find Chloe," Ella said, her eyes bright.

I turned to Gail hopefully.

She folded her arms, a dark expression on her face. "Oh, I can share my spell with you... but you have to do something for me first."

"What? But you said you didn't want another mother to go through—"

"I said I wouldn't put another mother through what I'd been through," Gail corrected. "But I also heard enough at that... party to know that this Chloe girl isn't right in the head. She probably ran off like that boy suggested. So. You find out what happened to Penelope and I'll give you the spell."

I fisted my hands together. "Chloe's life could be in danger. I promise I'll look for Penelope, but you need to give us the spell first!"

Gail gave me a hard grin. "No. I really don't."

She disappeared, giving herself the last word. I groaned as I threw myself back against my seat, covering my face.

"What happened?" Ella asked.

"She will not help unless we find out what happened to Penelope Blackwood," I groaned. I lowered my hands again, frowning. "Abigail seemed to be cagey when I brought it up to her... maybe she knows more than she's letting on. Maybe we should look into—"

Liam grunted. "You mean look into her to find out what she knows when she has nothing to do with this case?"

I stared at him, confused at the hostile tone.

"That's exactly what I did with you... that you got angry at me for doing," he said, leaning forward.

Ella cleared her throat. "I think I should go... call David Blackwood and see if we can get into the museum."

I opened my mouth to protest—or beg her to stay here with me—but she scurried away too quickly. Which was just as well. I sighed heavily as I leaned my elbows on the table. It would be best for Liam and I to have an actual talk. We'd been interrupted before.

"So. If you're a witch, why couldn't you tell me about it?" Liam asked brusquely. "Beyond not thinking I'd believe you, I mean."

I traced the grains of wood on the table with a finger. "It's the number one rule for all witches. Tell no one. I wanted to tell you. If I hadn't been terrified for Ella's safety, I would have been relieved when you learned about it during the equinox. Only… then you hit your head."

"But why do you have to keep it a secret?"

"You know the history of witch hunts. You know how many people were killed for being witches," I said slowly, then lifted my gaze to his. He stared at me intently. "There are still witch hunters out there. They might not be officially sanctioned like they used to be, but they're there. And they still kill witches."

A furrow appeared between his eyes. "How? If people are running around burning other people at the stake—"

"You're a detective. How many people are murdered or go missing in a year? How many unsolved cases are there?" I demanded.

Liam was quiet for a long moment before he slowly nodded. "Alright. So you couldn't tell me because you were afraid for your safety. When I showed you those notes I was keeping on you… you were afraid it'd bring these witch hunters down on you?"

"It meant I wasn't being careful enough."

"Then maybe it's something you should consider with Abigail. If she's keeping secrets from you, maybe she has valid reasons, too. Besides, I don't see how she could have anything to do with any of this. She wasn't at the party, and as for Gail Blackwood, what could Abigail have to do with a ghost?"

"I… they have the same first name," I said weakly.

Liam gave me a look that clearly told me it wasn't good enough. "Lots of people are named Abigail. That doesn't mean they have anything to do with a specific Abigail that lived four hundred years ago."

He was right, of course. I had no reason to think that Abigail was connected to any of this, other than the vaguest notion that somehow she was a descendant of Gail. And really, was it at all likely that was the case? It didn't matter, either, not unless Abigail being alive somehow proved that Penelope had survived Howard Whitman.

Was I just using this as a reason to put more distance between Liam and me? I didn't know.

Liam cleared his throat. "We should focus on the case at hand. If you believe a ghost can help us find Chloe, then you should investigate how you see fit. I, for one, am going to follow the money. Angelica claims Chloe scammed Anabel. I got a copy of her finances while we were searching. She's been taking out five thousand dollars a month, cash."

"How did you get a copy of her finances so quickly?" I asked, stunned.

"I made a few calls while you were talking with Anabel." Liam leaned forward again. "I think Chloe was being blackmailed. And I think that it's related to her disappearance tonight. Money usually reveals the truth of what's happening in these places."

I folded my arms. "You mean like how it revealed Percival Whitman was using magic to attack people in January?"

He grinned at me. "It revealed Percival Whitman had reason to attack David Blackwood since David found proof that the Whitmans didn't own as much land as they claimed."

"Oh. Oh… that… actually makes a lot of sense," I said, stunned.

Liam nodded. "I'm going to track down where the money went."

"And I'm going to find out what happened to Penelope Blackwood, so I can get a searching spell," I replied. "My searching winds don't have enough range for me to run around looking for Chloe myself."

"Searching winds?"

I grinned at him and lifted my hands. "One of my proficiencies is with wind. I have different types. Ones that lift, ones that search, ones that warm, others that chill. I used my lifting winds to pull Anabel Marley out of the whispering well in May."

Liam grunted, looking somewhere between unconvinced and impressed. "Alright. Let me know what you find."

CHAPTER 5
THE SOLSTICE SPELL

The darkness pressed against the museum windows like a living thing. I stifled a yawn as the coffee pot finished percolating. I'd gotten the key from David Blackwood, but I was here at the museum all by myself. I couldn't help but feel a little creeped out, especially considering that it was here at the museum that Percival Whitman's frost wolves attacked me in January... and that it was now the hour of the wolf.

I poured myself a cup of coffee and took it back to the computer, where various digitized pages were sitting on the screen.

My tin of baked goods that Abigail had given me a couple days ago sat near the computer, and I dunked a donut into my coffee before biting into it. It was delicious, as all of Abigail's baking was. But it made me think about what Liam said, about Abigail keeping her secrets the same way I kept mine. He was right, of course. I had no reason to go poking around in her life.

I just had to wonder if Liam knew more about Abigail than he was letting on.

"Focus, Harper," I told myself sharply. I couldn't let myself keep getting distracted. Liam was right. It was highly unlikely that Abigail had any sort of connection to Gail. Besides, I'd found what I needed.

Reaching into my pack, I pulled out a handful of candles and a bell. I set them up in the proper order, then summoned my magic to light them all. David had had cameras installed in the museum, but they covered the doorways and windows. I was in the archives in the basement and there were no cameras down here.

"I summon Gail Blackwood," I said into the candle flames. "I have news for her."

Gail's face flashed in the center of the circle. Then she was standing next to me. She pulled her shawl tightly around her shoulders as I stood up to be level with her.

"Well? Did you find anything?" The hope was clear in her tone, though she eyed me with distrust.

"I did," I said.

Gail's eyes widened. She trembled and nodded at me to continue.

"It's been difficult, but I think I've found answers. There were several town announcements in a nearby town that have been preserved, as well as a handful of diaries. One of them belongs to someone who was called Abigail Churchill. Who I think is Penelope."

"What do you mean?"

I pointed at the digitized pages of the diary. "She was found wandering around in the snow around the time Penelope disappeared. She had no memory of what had brought her there. My guess is that Howard Whitman's spell stole her memories and deposited her somewhere else."

"But if she was that close, someone ought to have seen her at some point," Gail protested.

"Maybe they did, but she'd changed enough that they didn't recognize her. Maybe even her appearance changed, I don't know." I shook my head. "Your searching spells didn't work because Penelope didn't know herself anymore."

"That... could be it," Gail murmured.

"I've read through bits of all her diaries," I told Gail, softening my voice as I switched to a new page. "She had a thrilling, fulfilled life. And she must have felt some connection to her past still, otherwise, why would she name her new self after you?"

Gail was quiet as she leaned over the computer, her eyes skimming the page. "It... it looks like her writing."

"I don't think she's still here. I don't think she had unfinished business, Gail. I think she moved on," I told her gently. I couldn't imagine how hard it would be to exist in four hundred years of not knowing.

Gail sighed heavily, and a waft of warm wind fluttered through the archives. "You might be right... here. The searching spell."

She held a hand out to me. I pressed my palm to hers, surprised to find that she was solid beneath my touch. She closed her eyes, and a shock jumped from her palm to mine. Instantly, the details of the spell flooded my mind. Before I could process it all, she sighed again. She smiled as she faded from view, the warmth of her departure lingering.

"Gail?" I called.

No answer. But I didn't expect one. I somehow knew she was gone for good now.

I processed the spell she'd given me and frowned. It wasn't one that I could do on my own. Maybe I could ask Ella to help me... but no. I knew exactly what I had to do.

Liam looked around at the setup I'd put together. The candles, crystals, and other ritual equipment. It was the most intensive spell I'd ever performed. It might have sapped a great deal of energy from Gail every time she performed it.

"What do you need from me?" Liam asked doubtfully.

"Stand right here," I said, pulling him over to a spot in the intricate design I'd painted on the floor. I checked the time. "We'll have to get this done quickly. Once the dawn comes, it'll be too late to perform the spell."

Liam opened his mouth, then closed it.

"How this works is that we should get a vision of what led up to Chloe's disappearance and where she is now," I explained as I took my spot. The candles were already lit and the pulse of magic was in the air. My palms were clammy as I took Liam's hands in mine.

"I don't have magic, so how is this going to work?" Liam blurted.

"I only need you to say the words and give me your energy. Are you ready?"

Liam searched my face and nodded slowly.

"Okay. Together, then." I took a deep breath and started reciting the words, Liam speaking along with me. "While the darkness lingers, let us see. With the dawning of the sun, bring the dawning of the truth. I call on Chloe to find where she is."

Wind burst through the shop. My hair was whipped into my face, and then suddenly I was back at Anabel's house. Liam and I stood holding hands in the middle of the dance floor, where Chloe was slow dancing with Trevor. I glanced over my shoulder, seeing Liam and myself in the corner as we had been only a few hours ago.

"How...?" Liam said. His head swiveled this way and that.

"Magic," I told him.

Anabel came into the room and announced the fireworks. People passed through us as they filtered out. Liam shuddered, and I squeezed his hand. "Yeah, it's not a pleasant experience, is it? But we have to follow Chloe."

Liam craned his head. "This way."

We followed her out to the front yard, but as the fireworks started, she looked around with a concerned expression. When she turned back into the house, we followed.

"Trevor?" she called.

She headed through the house, peeking first into the living room before she heard voices in a closet. I crept after her, though I knew we were making no sound. Chloe pressed her ear to the door, while Liam and I could hear the voices inside clear as day.

"—she's realizing. We can't keep this secret forever," Angelica was saying.

"Trust me, she doesn't suspect a thing."

Liam growled under his breath as Chloe flung open the door. "They are having an affair, after all."

Chloe cried out, her fists clenched. "And just what secret are you talking about, Angelica?"

Angelica's face turned white. Trevor seized her hand. "Chloe, I'm sorry. Angelica and I are in love."

"I can't believe you. I trusted you!" Chloe spun on her heel. She didn't see Trevor leap forward—

Everything went black. Liam stumbled, gasping. He clutched my hand as he groaned. "We have to stop. It's too much—"

"We have to know what happened," I said, wrapping both my arms around him. Pressure built behind my eyes, making me feel like my head was going to explode. "Please, Liam. You're strong, you can hold on."

Flashes of streetlights blurred through the darkness. It made me feel nauseated, and I groaned, biting my lips together tightly to keep myself from vomiting. Liam's arms tightened around me; now he was the one holding me up.

"It will pass soon," he promised. "It's because of the blow to her head."

One streetlight slowed, and I realized we were actually in a car. Chloe was in the backseat, hands bound with a gag in her mouth. Angelica turned to stare at her, face cast in shadows. Chloe shied back, but then the door was opened. Trevor dragged her out and marched her up the stairs. The fireworks still banged somewhere in the distance.

Trevor and Angelica took Chloe into the house, where everything went dark again briefly. When the light came back, Chloe was chained to a radiator, staring up at a basement door while tears streaked down her face.

A gust of cold knocked into me. I gasped as my eyes flew open. The candles had melted down. A wave of dizziness passed over me and I slowly sagged to the ground, Liam with me. He panted, his face ashen. Then he ground his teeth together and grabbed my hand again.

"I know that house," he said. "We have to move."

I nodded, forcing myself back to my feet. My legs shook with every step, but I seemed to grow stronger as we got outside. The first pale streaks were showing in the eastern sky. Liam pulled me to his car and soon we were off.

"So they're the ones that took her, then made a fuss about her missing so they could seem innocent," I murmured. "And so they could make it seem like she just took off."

Liam nodded, his expression tight. "Something still doesn't feel right, though. The money Chloe withdrew from her account has to be part of it. But how?"

As I studied Liam's profile, a realization hit me. This wasn't based on facts. It was a hunch... I'd been misjudging him for a long time, thinking that just because he thought little magic, it meant he was all about practicality. But he wasn't. Sure, he was skeptical, but he also understood there were more things that he didn't understand.

So what if we were misjudging Trevor and Angelica too? They were awfully quick to admit to an affair when Chloe had no proof.

"Keeping a secret can be many things," I said slowly. The pieces clicked into place and I gasped. "They were lying. Everything they told us, and Chloe, was a lie. I know what really happened!"

CHAPTER 6
DAWN OF THE TRUTH

D awn broke by the time we reached Angelica's house. She must have seen us pull up because she was waiting at the door when Liam and I came racing up the drive.

"What are you doing here?" she snapped at us. "I'm tired. Please come back later."

Liam shook his head. "Can we come in? It's important. We believe Chloe might be in danger."

Angelica glared at the two of us. "Chloe is a flake that has flaked out on me for the last time. Please, come back later."

I held my hand open, sending my searching winds through the doorway. Angelica shivered as they brushed by her, but her attention was on Liam. I found the doorway leading to the basement quickly and slipped my winds beneath the door, tripping down the stairs. Chloe was awake, thank goodness. I used my winds to pull the gag from her mouth.

"It really is very important," Liam insisted.

Angelica opened her mouth again, but even as she did so, a faint cry rose out of the basement. "Help! Someone help me! They're going to kill me!"

Angelica jumped. Liam drew his taser and pushed his way into the house. "A cry for help, reason to answer."

A door slammed from the front yard, and Trevor raced toward us. "What do you think—"

He came to a stop as police sirens wailed. Angelica bolted down the stairs and I used my winds to trip them both, sending them sprawling, as the police cruisers pulled into the front yard. Liam grabbed my hand, and we raced for the basement door together.

"Harper," Liam said.

I knew what he wanted. I flung my hand, sending my strong winds forward. The basement door burst off its hinges and slipped down the stairs. We were quick after it, racing down. Chloe was a bloody mess, bound to radiator pipes with zip ties. She burst into tears as she saw us.

"Get the paramedics in here," Liam called to me.

He jumped down the stairs. I turned back to the front yard. Both Angelica and Trevor were being shoved into cruisers just as an ambulance pulled up.

"In here," I called. "We need medical attention."

Then I returned to the basement door, standing there to help guide the paramedics in. From where I stood, I could see Chloe bury her face in Liam's shoulder. She sobbed, clutching at him. And for the briefest, most insane moment... I felt jealous.

The paramedics came in and checked her out. She could walk under her own power to the ambulance. Liam rode with her, and I drove his car. Once at the hospital, he met me in the waiting room and took me to her room.

"You were right," he told me as we moved through the hallway. "Trevor and Angelica were stealing from her. They were worried she'd figure it out and hand them over to the police, so they kidnapped her. They figured they could drain her account and then get rid of her."

I shuddered. How awful would it be to learn that a friend was lying to you for your entire relationship? I winced and glanced guiltily at Liam from the corner of my eye.

"I'm sorry I lied to you," I whispered.

His gaze softened, and he touched my cheek. "You had every

reason to—and we'll talk about this more, Harper. I still don't know how I feel about all of this, but I know I still trust you."

Warmth blossomed through my chest. I smiled gratefully at him. He smiled back, then knocked on Chloe's door.

She was awake and sitting up when we came in. Chloe smiled stiffly at me.

"I understand you helped the detective find me," she said. "Thank you. I don't know what I'd do if… well. I'm just glad you found me."

"Angelica and Trevor won't be able to hurt you again," Liam promised. "They're going away for a long time."

Chloe nodded, letting out a shuddering breath. "Would it be too much to ask for you to stay with me for a little while? Just to be sure…?"

I grabbed two chairs and brought them over. I smiled at Chloe as I sat on one side of the bed, Liam on the other. "Why don't you tell us about what they were blackmailing you for?" I asked.

Chloe ducked her head. "It's all so stupid."

"They've already tried to cut a deal by claiming you're part of some sort of criminal activity," Liam offered. "It's best if you tell us the truth. But, I must advise you it's a good idea to have a lawyer here."

"But I'm innocent," Chloe protested.

Liam shook his head. "Innocent people need lawyers, too."

Chloe hesitated a moment, then shook her head. "I trust you. The truth is… the truth is, that business venture I had with Anabel? It didn't just go wrong. I lost everything, investing in the wrong thing. I couldn't admit it, so I hid the proof.

"Then one day I got a package, showing me all the details of what I'd done. Only, it made it look like I'd stolen the funds Anabel gave me. It was terrifying, and the message said if I gave them five thousand dollars, it would all go away. But it didn't. Every month, they demanded the same amount, which was practically my entire paycheck. I didn't know what to do."

Liam shook his head. "Which is what they were counting on."

Chloe sighed. "I guess it was. I feel like such an idiot. I should have known them better. And now…"

She closed her eyes. My gaze met Liam's. His expression softened as he gazed back at me. I sighed internally. Even if he wasn't angry anymore, we still had a lot to talk about.

———

"That feels like it was the longest morning of my life, let alone the year," Liam groaned as he sank onto the couch.

We were back at my apartment. My personal library of books lined every wall interspaced with the heirlooms my ancestors had left me. The couch was Abigail's old one; she recently bought herself a new set, and I bought her old furniture from her.

"So." I sat next to him. I'd wracked my brain for hours to find the perfect words, but there was only one thing I could ask. "Where do we go from here?"

Liam rested his hands on his knees. "It's only been six weeks since the spring equinox. And those six weeks have been... very difficult. I miss you, Harper. A lot."

He turned toward me. The bags under his eyes were dark, but his expression was earnest as he took a deep breath.

"I hate this. You can't know how much I've regretted that stupid notebook. I'm so sorry."

"No, don't be. You saw something weird and were concerned for me. I only wish I told you sooner."

Liam chuckled softly. "About magic."

"Yeah. About magic."

He laughed, shaking his head. "You know, even though I took part in that magic spell, I'm not sure I believe it actually happened."

"Oh." I leaned back, frowning. What did he mean by that? If he didn't believe it happened, what did he think happened? That I drugged him?

"Regardless, I care about you, Harper. Deeply." Liam searched my face, nerves breaking through his careful mask. "I won't tell anyone about this."

Warmth spread through my chest again. I nodded, unable to speak through the lump in my throat.

Liam stretched his arms over his head. "So. Now we have to talk about Abigail... did you still want to investigate her?"

I shook my head. "No. Absolutely not. You were right. She had nothing to do with what was happening, and I know that she's got a few secrets up her sleeve, but she's owed her privacy. She's a good friend, and if she has any heritage in Moonhaven... well, I'm sure she has a reason for not wanting anything to do with it."

"And as for Gail having the same name?" Liam winked at me. "You still think that was a clue?"

"Not for Chloe's case... but Penelope's, yeah," I admitted. "I told you how I found a diary from Abigail Churchill, who matches everything to be Penelope Blackwood."

"Yeah."

I smirked at him. "She married someone named Benjamin Thorne. They named their first daughter Abigail, and their son named his first daughter Abigail, all the way down to..."

"The Abigail Thorne we know?" Liam breathed, his eyes wide.

"Exactly."

Liam laughed. "I guess that wraps it all up nicely, doesn't it?"

"I guess so."

He held his arms out for a hug. I gratefully wrapped my arms around him. As we shared a tender hug, I let out a sigh of relief. Liam knew the truth and would keep my secret. We'd solved the case and saved Chloe.

Everything in Moonhaven was settled once more.

The End
Did you enjoy *Summer Vibes?*
Please consider rating it on Bookbub, Goodreads or your favorite retailers. Reviews help me reach new readers.

Read all the books in the Cozy Mystery Samplers.

Read all the stories
Jane and Kennedy Daniels Mysteries
Pine Grove Mysteries

Wilma Wade Holiday Mysteries
Mike and Maddie Mysteries
Mystic Moonhaven Mysteries
Annie Archer Paranormal Mysteries

Join my Newsletter for updates and giveaways!
www.daisylandishromance.com